SHOWDOWN AT SKULL CANYON

There was a range war brewing: cattle-men against farmers, a familiar kind of trouble. But when Slade rode into Oresta — and into a hail of bul-lets — he found things weren't that simple. He put a stop to the range war, all right; but then the outlaw who'd masterminded it struck again with dynamite blasts! Slade knew he was up against a devilishly clever en-emy — a killer who would throw the whole border country into a blood-bath to carry out his plans.

BRADFORD SCOTT

SHOWDOWN AT SKULL CANYON

Complete and Unabridged

LINFORD
Leicester

First published in the United States by
Pyramid Books

First Linford Edition
published 2021
by arrangement with
Golden West Literary Agency

A catalogue record for this book is available
from the British Library.

ISBN 978-1-78541-963-8

Published by
Ulverscroft Limited
Anstey, Leicestershire

Printed and bound in Great Britain by
TJ Books Ltd., Padstow, Cornwall

This book is printed on acid-free paper

1

James G. 'Jaggers' Dunn, the famous General Manager of the vast C, & P. Railroad system, was angry. He scowled out the window of the Winona, his palatial green-and-gold private car, hammered the table with a huge and hairy fist, snorted and rumbled.

From his seat, he could see the web of tracks of the only partially completed assembly yard which should have been finished weeks before. Farther to the west stretched the twin steel ribbons that were not nearly as far westward as he had planned them to be. This latest branch of the C. & P. was having trouble. Dunn swore with astonishing fluency.

Sam, his porter, cook, and general factotum, kept discreetly in the background. The old colored gent knew it was wise to stay in the clear when the boss was having one of his bobberty spells. Suddenly, however, he burst into speech.

'Boss man!' he cried. 'Look who's comin'!'

Jaggers turned and glanced out the other window. He leaped to his feet and nearly took the car door off its hinges as he went through it. Scorning the steps, he leaped to the ground with an agility that would have done credit to a man thirty years younger and fifty pounds lighter.

'Slade!' he bawled. 'Well, I'll be blankety-blank-blanked! If you ain't a sight for sore eyes, or any other kind of eyes! Light off! Light off! Am I glad to see you!'

Ranger Walt Slade, named by the Mexican peons of the Rio Grande river villages *El Halcón* — The Hawk — dismounted gracefully from Shadow, his great black horse, and smiled down at the stocky G.M. from his great height. Dunn thrust out his huge paw and they shook.

'How are you, Walt?' he said. 'Come on in, come on in! Wait, I'll have the horse cared for.' He let out a bellow, 'Ike!'

2

A man came running. Jaggers gestured to the tall black. 'Look after him and give him the best,' he ordered. The man stretched forth a hand.

'Don't touch him,' Slade warned in his deep, musical voice.

'Oh, horses and me — ' the other began. Then — he yelped with pain as fingers like rods of woven steel gripped his shoulder and jerked him back, just in time. Shadow's ears had flattened, his eyes rolled wickedly and his lip curled to show gleaming white teeth.

'Why don't you do as I tell you?' Slade said. 'Want to lose half your arm?'

'I think I've lost it anyhow,' Ike groaned, rubbing his bruised shoulder. 'I thought a railbender had grabbed me.' 'You'd have thought something worse had grabbed you in another second,' Slade said. He glanced at the fellow, liked his looks.

'All right, Shadow, he's okay,' he said.

Shadow's ears pricked forward, his lip lowered, and he craned his neck toward Ike, blowing softly through his nose. 'He

3

understood just what you said!' Ike marveled. 'Didn' he?'

'He did,' Slade replied. 'Don't worry about him anymore. He allows no one to touch him unless I give the word; but now he's your friend. Go ahead, he'll follow you.'

Dunn, who had been a grinning observer of the incident, remarked, 'Ike, folks who don't do what Walt tells them to usually collect bruises, or worse. Keep that in mind and don't argue with him.'

'Think I'm a darn fool?' Ike replied in injured tones as he headed for the nearby stable, Shadow pacing sedately behind him.

Dunn chuckled, led the way into his private car, and motioned Slade to a comfortable chair beside the wide window that faced westward.

'Sam,' he called, 'break out a bottle, put coffee on to heat, and fix us a snack.'

'Comin' up, Boss man,' Sam answered. 'How are you, Mr. Slade?'

'Fine as frog hair,' Slade replied, shaking hands with Sam, an old friend. 'And

4

you?'

'Feelin' first rate now,' Sam said and hurried to his little kitchen. Dunn sat down and gazed expectantly at the Ranger. 'The governor received your letter and relayed it to Captain Jim,' Slade said, referring to Captain James McNelty, the famous Commander of the Border Battalion of the Texas Rangers. 'He figured I'd better amble over for a look-see. Gather you're up to your neck in trouble, per usual. What's the lowdown on the situation?'

'Oh, it's nothing new,' Dunn replied. 'Farmers have been pouring in and taking up land over to the west and south, lots of 'em. The cattlemen — this is, and always has been, cattle country, you know — don't like it. They call 'em nesters, which they aren't. They bought the land from the state and paid for it. But the cowmen say that land has always been open range and should have stayed that way. Understand?'

Slade nodded thoughtfully. No, it was not new. It had happened before in

5

Texas, but had been and could be the cause of serious trouble.

'The cowmen have been snipin' at them in various ways, but those farmers are mostly from Virginia and Kentucky and they fight back,' Dunn resumed. 'The cowmen know, of course, that this feeder is to service the farmers and have been doing all they can to delay construction and have been too blasted successful, so far.'

'Sure it's the cowmen?' Slade asked, gazing toward the dark and rugged hills shouldering the blue of the Texas sky to the north.

'Who else?' Dunn retorted.

'I don't know,' Slade answered frankly, 'but I've found that things aren't always just what they appear on the surface, as you should know.'

The G.M. grunted. 'Well, in this case — '

Boom!

2

The window panes jangled and the long coach rocked slightly on its springs.

Slade whirled to the window. Several hundred yards to the west, yellowish smoke was mushrooming. A big steam shovel lay on its side, spouting a white cloud from broken pipes. Men were scurrying about like disturbed ants.

'There's a sample!' howled Dunn leaping to his feet. 'And it ain't the first time! Come on, let's see how many got killed.'

Together they hurried to the scene of the explosion.

Fortunately — almost miraculously, Slade thought — nobody had gotten killed. The steam shovel operator was sitting on a crosstie, holding his bloody head in his hands and swearing with a vigor that discounted serious injury. Several track workers had been cut and bruised, none very badly. Everybody was keeping well away from the still smoking crater excavated by the exploding dynamite.

Slade walked to the edge of the shallow hole and peered into its depths.

'A couple of sticks, I'd say,' he remarked to Dunn, who was doing a better job of swearing than the injured shovel operator. 'Stuck full of percussion caps, the chances are, so that if anything hit them, off they'd go. Could easily have resulted in a killing. A wonder it didn't. And you say this has happened before?'

'Something like it,' Dunn replied. 'Last week they blew up a switch engine and just about wrecked it. But it isn't the property damage that counts, it's the slowing up of the work. Every time the boys stick a pick in the ground they jump, and they try to examine the ground before tackling it. Who can blame them!' He turned to the injured men.

'Head for the cook shanty and get patched up. Then knock off for the rest of the day,' he told them. 'We'll get the doctor from town to look you over.'

Slade gazed toward the huddle of buildings a little less than a half mile to the west by a bit south.

'That's Oresta over there, is it not?' he asked.

'That's right,' said Dunn. 'An old-time cow town. There's another one, Hamon, about twelve miles farther to the west and south, where the farmers do their buying. Well, guess we might as well get back to the coach and see what Sam has fixed for us. Just a minute.'

He beckoned a man who, Slade judged, was a foreman, and gave orders to clean up the mess and get things moving.

The 'snack' Sam had prepared was more in the nature of a high-power full meal. Slade, who had found good food scarce of late, did it full justice. After eating, he rolled a cigarette, leaned back comfortably in his chair, and regarded the general manager.

Dunn eyed him in return, and thought what a splendid looking man Slade was. Very tall, more than six feet, he had wide shoulders and a broad chest that slimmed down to a lean, sinewy waist.

Dunn had always thought Slade's deeply bronzed face singularly arresting, with its rather wide mouth, grin-quirked at the corners, relieving somewhat the tinge of fierceness evinced by the prominent hawk nose above and the lean, powerful jaw and chin beneath.

The sternly handsome countenance was dominated by black-lashed eyes of very pale gray, cold, reckless eyes that nevertheless most always seemed to have little devils of laughter dancing in their clear depths.

But those devils, Jaggers Dunn well knew, could, did occasion warrant, be anything but laughing and the eyes would become like ice over fire.

A broad forehead was surmounted by thick, crisp hair, so black that in certain lights a blue shadow seemed to lie upon it.

Slade wore the homely, efficient garb of the range — bib-less overalls favored by cowhands, soft blue shirt with vivid neckerchief looped at his throat, scuffed half-boots of softly tanned leather, and broad-brimmed, somewhat battered 'J.B.,' — and he wore it as Richard the Lion-Hearted must have worn armor.

Around his waist were double cartridge belts, from the carefully worked and oiled cut-out holsters of which protruded the plain black butts of heavy guns. And from the butts of those big Colts his slender, powerful hands seemed never far away.

Altogether, Jaggers Dunn thought, a man to like, respect, depend on, and reckon with.

And, incidentally, a man the shrewd old general manager had proven several times before.

Walt Slade, before setting out on the long and hard ride to the railhead, had as near as was possible learned everything concerning the C. & P. Railroad. Suddenly he shot an indirect question at the G.M. 'Don't suppose you could perhaps be planning to build on across into New Mexico and west to Randal?'

Dunn jumped in his chair. 'Now

what the devil makes you say that?' he demanded.

'Guesswork,' Slade replied smiling.

'You and your blasted guesswork!' snorted Dunn. 'It always seems too darn near to being right. Yes, although it's supposed to be a dead secret — Hamon is supposed to be our terminus — we do plan to build on, fast, to Randal. There are some fat mail and express contracts to be picked up at Randal, and an almost virgin cattle and agricultural products country to be tapped.

'Now what the devil's on your mind?' he demanded, for Slade had smiled slightly, the devils of laughter edging to the front.

'Oh, nothing,' *El Halcón* replied, 'except that, as you must know, the M.K. is building west about forty miles to the south of here.'

The M.K. was a rival road, not noted for strictly ethical practices, with which Jaggers Dunn had tangled more than once.

'And you figure they might turn north?'

he asked. 'Would be a long and hard haul for them, while we have a straight and comparatively easy shoot west.'

'Yes, but were you delayed sufficiently, the difference in distance and terrain wouldn't matter much.'

'Blast it! You've got me worried!' Dunn exploded. 'Walt, have you heard something?'

Slade shook his bead.

'Nope,' he replied, 'it's just that I know how the M.K. crowd thinks and operates. Remember what happened down at Presidio.'

'When did you figure this thing out?' Dunn asked. 'Didn't exactly figure it,' Slade answered. 'It sort of came to me while I was looking into that hole the dynamite excavated. As I said before, that could easily have resulted in a killing — a wonder it didn't. And I got to wondering would the cattlemen risk murder just in taking out spite on you and the road. For they must know that though they can delay you, cause you trouble and expense, they can't stop you.'

'I see,' Dunn said slowly. 'But somehow I can't see the M.K. officials going to the length of murder. They've pulled some rather shady deals, but murder is something else again.'

'Granted,' Slade said. 'But sometimes an employee gets out of hand. That sort can't always be depended on to keep within reasonable limits. That happened at Presidio, you will recall. A fellow hired to do dirty work got completely out of hand and went it on his own. Could happen here.'

'Then you absolve the cowmen?'

'I didn't say that,' Slade denied. 'Cowmen are like any body else — there are good ones and there are bad ones. Not beyond the realm of possibility that one or more might be in cahoots with the M.K. bunch, in their pay, Of course, sir, all this is the purest guesswork on my part and I could be altogether wrong. Because of which I would not wish to have our conversation go beyond this car, which you can under stand.'

'Uh-huh, that I understand,' growled

the G.M. 'But what I can't understand is how you thought it all out so quickly.'

'It is my business to think such things out, just as it is your business to concentrate on running a railroad. To you, other matters are incidental. I was sent here to investigate certain overt acts. And right before my eyes, as it were, a criminal act was committed, which, I repeat again, might well have been accompanied by murder. I can't overlook any of the angles, all of which must be considered and investigated. So everybody who could possibly benefit in any way must be considered suspect, nobody dismissed or discounted until the chore is finished and those responsible for criminal acts brought to justice. Where you and I are concerned, the personal element enters into the picture as well as the effect such acts have on your project. Otherwise, I am a Texas Ranger, not a railroad builder.'

'Yes, but you are a darn sight better railroad builder and engineer than nine-tenths of those who consider themselves such,' grunted Dunn.

Jaggers Dunn was right. Shortly before the death of his father, which followed close on the heels of financial reverses that entailed the loss of the elder Slade's ranch, young Walt had graduated from a noted college of engineering. He had planned to take a postgraduate course in special subjects to round out his education and better fit him for the profession of engineering.

This, however, was impossible at the time, so when Captain McNelty, with whom he had worked during summer vacations, suggested that he sign up with the Rangers for a while and pursue his studies in spare time, Slade thought the idea a good one.

Long since he had gotten more from private study than he could have hoped for from postgrad courses and was eminently fitted to take up the profession he had determined would be his life work.

But things don't always work out as planned. Slade realized that Ranger work had gotten a strong hold on him, providing as it did so many opportunities to right wrongs, help deserving people, and make the land he loved a better place in which to live. He was reluctant to sever connections with the illustrious body of law enforcement officers. Plenty of time to be an engineer — he was young. He'd stick with the Rangers for a while.

After his pronunciamento, Jaggers fell silent, still regarding his table companion. Walt Slade had been his close associate for years and he knew when it was best to refrain from conversation. He knew Slade had something on his mind which he would reveal when ready and not before. It came in the nature of a question.

'Don't you have guards on the job here at night?'

'Yes,' growled Dunn, 'and lots of good they do. Chasin' their tails around in circles and getting no results. The hellions pull things right under their nose, or noses, rather. However, nothing I would call really serious happened until that locomotive was blown up about ten days back, which caused me to send the governor a wire and a letter. I figured that was going a mite too far and that something had to be done about it. What happened today was even worse.'

Slade nodded his understanding. Dunn's railroad police were all right when it came to keeping order and breaking up shindigs, but they were city men and the shrewd and ruthless brand of outlaw that usually worked in such a section as this was beyond their ken and experience.

'Emery dust in journal boxes, brake cylinders bored to let the air out, spikes pulled so rails are loose and engines and cars set on the ground, such things as that,' Dunn continued. 'Nothing really bad, but productive of plenty of delay in construction.'

'I see,' Slade said thoughtfully. 'Looks like the work of somebody with a knowledge of railroad machinery not usually found among cowhands.'

'Guess you're right there,' Dunn admitted.

'The way that dynamite was planted ahead of the shovel showed careful planning and foresight,' Slade added. 'They would have to know just where the shovel would be called into play to get results.'

'They got results, all right,' Dunn snorted.

Slade nodded and gazed north to where the brush-covered slopes, the naked rock, the crags and pinnacles of the range of hills showed even more sinister in the deepening twilight. He gestured toward the rugged range.

'The Tonto Hills,' he said, 'with the Tonto Desert beyond. That is and always has been outlaw land. Gentlemen who hang out there may also resent the coming of the railroad, which usually is accompanied, sooner or later, by law and order.'

'Guess that's so,' Dunn conceded. 'Now what are you getting at?'

'Oh, nothing definite,' Slade replied evasively. 'Just an other of the angles that also must not be overlooked. Well, I think I'll take a ride over to Oresta.

Understand it's quite a town.'

'A blasted hell-town,' rumbled Dunn. 'Always something bustin' loose. Several of my boys got cracked heads there. Another way to delay construction, I reckon.'

Slade did not argue the point although he doubted it was so. The railroad builders were a turbulent lot and usually such injuries were the results of their own misbehavior.

'You'll sleep here, of course. Won't be the first time,' Dunn added as the Ranger stood up. 'If you're still asleep when I get up, I'll go out through the kitchen so as not to disturb you. Be careful, now.'

'I will be,' Slade promised carelessly. He got the rig on Shadow and blithely rode to a date with trouble.

3

Oresta was quite a town, all right, for it serviced a wide and otherwise isolated though prosperous stretch of cattle country. Shipping herds from the north, west, and south paused there in the course of their more than seventy-mile drive east to the railroad loading pens.

The fact that the coming of the railroad to Oresta would greatly shorten the drive, to their profit, apparently carried little weight with the local cowmen. They were, Slade knew, largely creatures of habit who looked with disfavor upon innovations of any kind. Their fathers and their grandfathers had made that drive, so it was the proper thing to do.

That they would gradually alter their opinion was certain, but it would take time. So Jaggers Dunn might be right in his contention that it was the opposition of the cowmen of the section that was responsible for the delaying tactics used against him. Slade wasn't so sure. He glanced once more toward the grim hills to the north.

Although it was still early, Oresta was already going strong when Slade rode into town. Long lines of cow ponies stood at the hitch racks. There was a jostling crowd on the principal streets. Every other building, it seemed, housed a saloon.

Slade found a place at the rack in front of a big, brightly lighted and noisy saloon. He dismounted and dropped the split reins to the ground, all that was necessary to keep Shadow right where he was.

'I'll see you soon,' he promised. 'If I decide to stay late, I'll stable you, so take it easy for a spell and don't go getting your mad up.'

The big black did not deign to reply and to all appearances immediately went to sleep. Slade chuckled, and entered the saloon.

Something was going on near the center of the long bar. Slade deftly eased his way through the crowd until he could see what it was.

A ring of laughing cowboys surrounded two figures. One was a big and hulking young puncher more than half drunk. The other was an old Mexican with whom he was evidently having sport.

'Pap,' he rumbled hoarsely, 'I'm going to interdooce you to the bullet dance.' With which he drew a gun and fired a shot into the floor close to the Mexican's feet.

The old fellow yelped and capered with fright but could not escape because of the crowd hemming him in.

The puncher guffawed and took aim. His hand was none too steady and the old man might easily have lost a couple of toes.

But before he could pull trigger a second time, slender, steely fingers coiled about his wrist and forced the gun muzzle down. He yelled with pain as *El Halcón's* terrible grip ground the bones together. The gun thudded to the floor.

Bellowing curses, he twisted around and launched a blow at Slade's face. Before it had travelled six inches it was blocked. Then Slade gripped him by his shirt front and sent him hurtling through the air. He knocked over two chairs and a table before hitting the floor, and staying there.

His companions uttered angry cries, then fell silent as Slade swung around to face them. His eyes were the color of glacier ice, the thumbs of his hands were hooked over his double cartridge belts, directly above the out flaring butts of the big Colts. He spoke, his voice quiet but edged with steel.

'Not a very nice thing to do,' he said. 'Scaring an old man half out of his wits and taking a chance of crippling him.'

Under the searing contempt of the quiet voice, the cowboys flushed, glanced shame-facedly at one another. One spoke. 'Feller,' he said, apologetically, 'I guess you're right. That horned toad is always doing some loco thing he thinks is funny. He didn't mean to hurt the old jigger. But, blazes!

I'm scairt you've killed him; he ain't moved.'

'I doubt it,' Slade replied. 'His kind doesn't kill easy.

Throw some water over him and he'll come out of it.'

He turned to the Mexican, who apparently was frozen to the spot, and the cold eyes were abruptly all kindness as he addressed him in Spanish.

'*Amigo*, I don't think he meant any real harm, but be was behind the door when they were handing out brains.'

The old man stared at him, his eyes suddenly wide. Then he bowed low.

'*El Halcón*!' he exclaimed in a low voice. ' *El Halcón*, the friend of the lowly! Now will all be well!'

With another bow he turned and shuffled out the door. Slade started to approach the bar, but the cowboys, grinning, blocked him off.

'No you don't!' chuckled the one who had spoken. 'Feller, you can't buy. You've got to have a coupla snorts on us, just to show you we ain't a bunch of wind spiders.'

Slade regarded him a moment, then he smiled, the flashing white smile of *El Halcón* that men, and women, found irresistible.

'Thank you,' he accepted.

The punchers grinned more broadly and bobbed their heads. 'Feller, my name's Weston, Bill Weston' the spokesman introduced himself. 'I don't believe I caught your handle.'

Slade supplied it. The other rattled off half a dozen names and they shook hands all around.

'See they've got Hunch on his feet and he's soakin' wet,' Weston chuckled. 'Lafe Moore, the owner — the big feller with the red hair — is givin' him a stiff talkin' to. Lafe don't like to have ruckuses in his place. Well, here's how!'

Meanwhile, a tall, straight-featured man with dark blue eyes remarked to a drinking companion who had been standing close to the old Mexican when Slade spoke to him, 'Wonder who that big devil is anyhow?'

'Didn't you hear what the Mex said, Mr. Becker?' the other replied. 'That's *El Halcón*.'

'*El Halcón?*'

'Yep. Just about the saltiest owlhoot in Texas, or so a lot of folks will tell you, who's too blasted smart to ever get caught. He's always hornin' in on good things other folks have started, and skimmin' off the cream. And there's something else they say about him, too — 'The singingest man in the whole Southwest, with the fastest gunhand.' Yep, he's *El Halcón*, all right. I never saw him before, but I've heard tell what he looks like. He's bad.'

Becker gazed fixedly at Slade for a moment. 'Could be,' he conceded. Tossing off his drink, he nodded to the other and left the saloon.

Hunch, the skylarking puncher, came wobbling to the bar, looking decidedly subdued. Apparently he held no rancor for his chastisement at Slade's hands, for he greeted him with a somewhat watery grin.

27

'Feller, how in blazes did you do it?' he asked plaintively. 'I thought for a minute I'd done growed wings.'

'Guess I caught you off balance,' *El Halcón* smiled. The others roared with laughter.

'Uh-buh, you caught him off balance, all right,' chortled Weston.

'And it looked like the balance of him was going to splatter the floor with grease. Wouldn't have done no harm; he could lose a few pounds of tallow and not be hurt by it. Have a drink, Hunch? Figure you can still hold one?'

'I'll try,' accepted Hunch. 'May lose some of it, though; feel sorta leaky at the seams.' More laughter.

'Here comes the sheriff!' exclaimed Weston. 'He looks mad.'

The lanky old gent with a drooping mustache did not appear to be in a good mood. He strode straight to the group surrounding Slade, eyeing them with frank disapproval.

'Well, what was it?' he demanded harshly. 'I heard there was a shootin' in here.'

'A gentleman dropped his gun,' Slade replied mildly, with perfect truth. Snickers — sounded behind him. The sheriff did not appear impressed.

'Yeah, I reckon he did,' he said sarcastically. 'You Boxed C hellions are always startin' something. Some day I'm going to fill the calaboose so full with you, you'll hafta spit up in the air.' He turned to Slade.

'Stranger?' he stated rather than asked.

'Depends on one's interpretation of the word,' Slade replied.

'Huh! What's that?'

'Stranger, a person with whom one is unacquainted,' Slade quoted. 'Being acquainted with quite a few gents here, I hardly fit into that category.'

'Uh-huh, plumb close acquainted,' put in Hunch, amid more snickers.

'It ain't no rec'mendation,' the sheriff declared heartily. 'This is as ornery a bunch of horned toads as ever crawled out of the brush. You'd do well to steer clear of 'em. They'll take the gold fillin's

29

out of your teeth so slick you'll never miss 'em till you try to chaw.'

'I'll risk it,' Slade said, smiling to show he had no fillings. 'Everybody to their taste,' grunted the sheriff. 'But they sure leave a bad taste in my mouth. All right, let's not have any more goings on.' He turned to go but Slade laid a hand on his shoulder.

'Have a drink with us first, Sheriff,' he invited. 'May serve to take some of the bad taste out of your mouth.'

The sheriff tried to scowl, but the laughter in Slade's eyes caused him to grin instead. Rather crustily, but a grin nevertheless.

'Okay,' he accepted. 'I feel sorta reckless tonight, Willing to take a chance on getting pizened.' He turned to Weston.

'How's the Old Man, Bill?' he asked.

'He's coming along,' replied Weston. 'Arm is still a mite sore but it's on the mend and don't bother him too much.' 'Glad to hear it,' said the sheriff raising his glass to Slade. 'Tom Carvel is all right, even if he ain't overly pertick'ler in what he hires to ride for him.'

'The Old Man got a slug through his arm a coupla weeks back,' Weston explained to Slade.

'How's that?' the Ranger asked.

'Some sidewinder threw down on him from the brush,' Weston answered. 'A wonder he wasn't drilled dead center.' Any notion as to who did it?' Slade asked casually. Weston scowled.

'One of the blasted nesters over to the west, of course,' he replied. Slade nodded; he'd learn more about that later. 'Oh, by the way,' said Weston. 'Slade, this is Sheriff Brad Orton. Sheriff, this is Walt Slade, a good *hombre.*'

'In bad company,' said the sheriff as he shook hands. He finished his drink.

'Okay, boys,' he said. 'Try and not drop any more guns.

I crave peace and quiet.' With which he stalked out.

'He's all right,' Weston remarked. 'Can't blame him for getting riled now and then; he's got troubles.'

Which last, Slade felt, was a prime

31

example of understatement.

Lafe Moore, the owner, came over and was introduced. 'I kept out of it till Orton left,' he said. 'Figured Slade could handle things, after the way he handled Hunch.' He scowled at the still damp puncher.

'Why in blazes do you always have to be doing something you shouldn't,' he demanded.

'I was just playin',' Hunch protested.

'Guns are not good things to play with,' Slade interpolated. 'Folks have been known to be hurt by them.' Loud laughter followed. Hunch looked sheep-ish.

'Uh-huh, and they get hurt by other things 'sides guns,' he said, furtively rubbing a bruised shoulder.

'Well, have one on the house,' invited Moore. 'And much obliged to you, Mr. Slade. Hope you'll see fit to drop in often. Here come the girls. Maybe they will keep you young helm lions occupied for a while.'

With a smile and a nod he moved to

the far end of the bar.

'His girls are good lookers, and nice,' Weston remarked, gazing appreciatively toward the dance — floor which was now occupied. 'Lafe won't have any other kind. Insists they be squareshooters. Same goes for his dealers and barkeeps. He runs a straight place and does about the best business in town. More'n you can say for some of the rum holes here abouts. As Orton said, there are places where they'll take the fillin's outa your teeth without you knowin' it, and then maybe sell 'em back to you before you realize they're your own.' He chuckled, sampled his glass and continued.

'This has always been a wild town, like Fort Worth and Tascosa and other places like that where the trail herds lay over. Now with the railroad shovin' this way she's gettin' even wilder. Tomorrow a couple of big herds will roll in from the southwest and tomorrow night she'll really jump. Figure to coil your twine here for a spell?'

'Probably, for a spell,' Slade replied.

He had let Weston run on without interruption for he figured he was getting something of a lowdown on conditions from the garrulous puncher's chatter. He resolved to try a question or two.

'There's been serious trouble between the cowmen and the farmers?'

Weston glanced about. Some of his companions were on the dance-floor. Others were conversing with acquaintances along the bar. He lowered his voice.

'Yes, there has,' he said. 'Between you and me, I figure there's a lot of darn foolishness on both sides. You know how the old-timers are about what's always been open range and what they figure always should be. Having it bought up didn't set well with them. Of course the farmers heard of how they felt about it, and *they* came in with chips on their shoulders. They're a purty salty lot from the Kentucky, Virginia, and Tennessee hill country. There was quite a bit of bickerin' and snipin' back and forth from the beginning.'

He paused to take a drink, then added,

'Sorta funny, though, there wasn't any real trouble till a coupla months back; then it started. Cowhands have been shot at, especially up toward the hills to the north. A couple of them got plugged, not serious, but they didn't feel over good about it. The farmers say they've been shot at, too. Maybe they have. I do happen to know that one of 'em got purty bad hurt somehow — doctor had trouble pullin' him through. They had a couple of haystacks and a barn burned. That made 'em good and mad and they turned a creek that several of the west pastures depend on for water leavin' 'em high and dry, and you can't raise cows without water. There was a row here in town — some of 'em come here when they take a notion. They're an independent lot and won't be fenced out, even though this has always been a cow town. Sheriff Orton and his deputies had got wind of what might happen and managed to bust it up 'fore it turned into a real corpse and cartridge session.

'Those are samples of what's been

going on. And, as I told you, the Old Man got one through his arm. He's a sorta big jigger in this section — the Boxed C is top range hereabouts and that sure got the other owners on the prod.'

'I see,' Slade remarked thoughtfully. 'And you say that only in the past few months has really bad trouble developed?'

'That's right,' answered Weston. 'Before that there wasn't anything really bad happened. Things build up that way, though, and all of a sudden bust loose.'

'And the cattlemen resent the coming of the railroad?'

'Yep, the old-timers do,' Weston admitted.

'They say the road will bring in all sorts of riff-raff, and more farmers. That the engines scare the fat off the cows and the sparks set things afire. They tried to stop it from coming, and failed up. The railroad went to court and invoked, what do you call it, Eminent Domain?' Slade nodded.

'So the road got the right to go

through,' Weston resumed. 'The way things are going, I'm scairt all hell is liable to bust loose, sooner or later. Used to be a plumb peaceful section.'

4

Slade nodded his understanding. It was a condition all too prevalent in Texas. For many years, the big ranch owners had lived a life comparable to that of the feudal barons of the Middle Ages. From their 'castle' strongholds they had ruled wide stretches of country, where their word was law. They resented any interference with the prerogatives they had relegated to themselves and had put down encroachments with a heavy hand.

But that was changing. Immigrants from the east were pouring in, taking up land, making homes, building their own towns, challenging the dominance of the cattle barons. As a result, there had been, and still would be, violence and bloodshed. Looked like what was happening here followed a familiar pattern.

But Slade was not so sure. It seemed to him that the methods employed denoted an originality foreign to cattle land. Well, the fact remained that lawless acts were being committed, and it was his chore as a Texas Ranger to prevent those acts and bring the perpetrators to justice. And he had no intention of slighting the chore, no matter who suffered in consequence.

Sheriff Orton appears to be a good man,' he observed.

'He is,' said Weston. 'He's okay when it comes to bustin' up ruckuses and dropping his loop on cow thieves and such. Oh, we've got 'em here. New Mexico and the hills and markets for widelooped beefs ain't far off. But I'm scairt that now he's up against something that's too much for him. I figure we're darn likely to get a bunch of Rangers here to straighten things out.' Slade smiled and didn't comment.

'So you see what you've ambled into' Weston grinned.

'Chuck-line riding?'

'When I happen to be,' Slade answered with a smile. Weston scratched his head.

'I can't exactly figure that one,' he confessed. 'Gather, though, that you mean

39

when you are you are and when you ain't you ain't. Right?'

'That will be close enough,' Slade smiled.

Weston chuckled. 'Let's have another drink,' he suggested.

'If you don't mind,' Slade said, 'I think I'll try and find a vacant table and settle for some coffee. First, though, I wish to stall my horse. I promised I would if I decided to stay here any length of time and he'll be swearing if I don't keep my word. Can you tell me where I can locate a stable?'

'I'll show you,' Weston volunteered. 'Guess I'd better corral my cayuse, too. Looks like I'm hogtied here for a while.'

They left the saloon together and approached the hitch rack.

'Just a hop and a skip, but I reckon we might as well ride,' Weston said.

Knowing the average cowhand's aversion to walking when he didn't absolutely have to, Slade offered no objection. He swung into the saddle. Weston forked his own mount and they rode slowly along the crowded street.

'Here it is,' Weston said, after they had covered several blocks. 'Right down the alley a little ways.' He turned into a shadowy and narrow opening between two buildings.

As usual, Slade took careful note of his surroundings as they approached the stable. He noticed that about a half score paces from the door they passed under a fairly large tree that grew against one of the building walls, its branches casting a dark shadow across the ground.

The door was opened by a cheerful and corpulent individual who greeted Weston by name, exclaimed over Shadow, and was properly introduced to the big black.

Slade made sure all Shadow's wants were cared for. Then he and Weston left the stable. His keen hearing caught the click of a bolt as the keeper locked the door. They turned and started back the way they had come.

Suddenly Slade's long arm flashed out and swept Weston off his feet. In

41

the same ripple of motion he went sideways along the building wall, weaving, ducking, both guns blazing answer to the flickers of flame gushing from under the tree. There was a wailing cry and a form pitched forward into view to lie motionless. A slug twitched Slade's shirt sleeve like an urgent hand. A second just grained the flesh of his left thigh. Then a second shadowy figure slumped, to the ground.

Guns ready for instant action, Slade glided forward. A single swift glance told him the two drygulchers were dead. He whirled and sped back to Weston who was back on his feet, raving profanity. Slade seized him by the arm.

'To the other end of the alley!' he snapped, dragging Weston along with him. Another moment and he halted at the far mouth of the narrow lane, some fifty yards from where the two bodies lay.

'What — what in blazes!' gasped Weston.

'Take it easy,' Slade told him. 'Stay right where you are. The shooting must have been heard on the street and there'll be folks coming to see about it before long. And listen, Bill, do me a favor, will you?"

'I'd sure be an ungrateful vinegarroon if I didn't,' the cowboy panted. 'You saved my life, sure as blazes. Those first slugs passed right through where I was standing 'fore you slapped me down. And you risked your own life taking time to do it. Those blasted nesters are really getting bad. Aiming to even up some score, I reckon.'

'You think they were farmers?' Slade asked.

'I'll bet a hatful of pesos they were,' the cowhand declared.

'Better scale that down to one busted peso,' Slade advised dryly.

'You don't think so?'

'I do not,' Slade answered. 'Not the way they are dressed and the way they handled their irons. I don't know what this is all about, but I'll do the betting they were not farmers.'

Weston swore pungently. 'What's the

favor you were going to ask?' he said.

'That you won't mention what happened tonight until I give the word,' Slade said. 'I have my reasons for asking.'

'Okay,' said Weston. 'The latigo's tight on my jaw. How in blazes did you catch on so fast?'

'I saw them beneath the tree, saw the glint of metal as they shifted their guns to line sights,' Slade explained, not pointing out that it was his remarkable eyesight and his marvelous coordination of mind and muscle that had saved them. Weston swore some more as Slade began ejecting the spent shells from his Colts and replacing them with fresh cartridges.

'I didn't see anything,' he said. 'And I never saw such shootin'. Those guns just happened in your hands. Look! Here comes some folks.'

Heads were poking cautiously around the corners at the far end of the alley. Men came into view, easing forward slowly. Soon they were grouped around the bodies. More and more followed them.

'Okay, let's go and see what we bagged,' Slade suggested. 'Work in with the others and we won't be noticed,'

They sauntered down the alley and a few moments later had joined the group around the bodies, which were clothed in rangeland garb.

'Take a good look at their faces and see if you recognize them,' Slade breathed to his companion.

Weston did so, peering close. He shook his head.

Wild conjectures were flying about as to what was the reason for the double killing. The consensus seemed to be that the two had had a falling out of some sort and had gunned each other. If anybody recognized the unsavory looking pair they refrained from saying so.

'Let's go,' Slade said as more and more men crowded into the alley. 'Sheriff should be showing up shortly.'

'And I don't want to tangle with him,' muttered Weston as they headed for Moore's saloon. 'He's sorta smart and if he got to askin' me questions I might let something slip. Ornery looking scorpions, weren't they?'

'About average, I'd say,' Slade replied. He would have liked to examine the bodies more thoroughly, but that was hardly practical, under the circumstances. Perhaps he would be able to get something out of the sheriff, later.

He did. A surprise.

5

They reached Moore's place, which boasted the somewhat ominous soubriquet of The Widow Maker, and found it going strong. Slade spotted a vacant table near the dance-floor, sat down, and ordered coffee and a sandwich. Weston joined his fellow punchers at the bar for the time being.

Men who had visited the alley began drifting in and soon the double killing was the prime topic of conversation. Shortly, however, the subject was dropped. Gun fights in Oresta were too frequent an occurrence to admit of lengthy debate. For the eyes of the girls were bright, the drinks good and strong, and youth and lusty life are not wont to dwell for long on death and what comes after.

Slade was sipping his coffee when Sheriff Orton sauntered in, glanced about, and approached the table.

'Sit down and have a drink,' the Ranger

invited.

'Think I'll settle for coffee, same as you,' said Orton as he occupied a chair. He regarded Slade severely after the waiter had taken his order.

'Been hearing things about you, young feller,' he said.

'Hear you have another name 'sides Slade.'

'Yes?'

'Yes — *El Halcón*.'

'Been called that,' Slade admitted and waited for the explosion.

It didn't come. The sheriff grinned and twinkled his eyes at him.

'Was over to El Paso County a while back,' he remarked reminiscently, 'Conflabbin' with the sheriff over there. Some how we got to discussin' *El Halcón*.'

'What did he tell you?' Slade asked.

'Nothing he shouldn't have,' answered Orton. 'Only the way he talked you up got me to sorta wondering. So I did a mite of investigating, put two and two together and made five. How's old Jim McNelty? I used to know him quite well.'

'He's fine,' Slade replied, adding, 'And I guess you understand why I prefer to be known here only as *El Halcón*, if possible.'

'I understand,' nodded the sheriff. 'Don't worry about me — I ain't a blabbermouth. And I'm sure glad Jim sent you here; things have been getting sorta out of hand. Just what did happen in that alley?'

Without reservation, Slade told him. Orton swore under his mustache.

'And you don't figure it was a couple of the nesters just gunnin' what they thought were some cowhands?'

'No, I don't,' Slade replied, 'and I don't think you do, either.'

'Guess you're right,' conceded the sheriff. 'I don't; but what's the meaning of it?'

'The meaning, I'd say,' Slade answered, 'is that somebody has recognized me as *El Halcón* and figures the quicker I'm gotten rid of, the better.'

'Puts you on a nice hot spot,' snorted the sheriff.

'I've been on similar spots, and they never amounted to much,' Slade replied carelessly.

Which was true.

Due to his habit of working undercover as much as possible and often not revealing his Ranger connections, Walt Slade had built up a peculiar dual reputation. Those who knew the truth declared vigorously he was not only the most fearless but the ablest of the Rangers. Others, including some puzzled sheriffs and marshals, who knew him only as *El Halcón*, a dangerous man with killings to his credit, maintained as vigorously that he was just a blasted owl hoot too smart to get caught, so far.

But the Mexican *peones* would say, ' *El Halcón*, the good, the just, the compassionate, the friend of the lowly. *El Dios, guard* him!'

Walt Slade was confident that so long as he proved worthy, their prayers would be answered. So he went his carefree way as *El Halcón* and worried about the future not at all.

Sheriff Orton knew, as did Captain McNelty, that his El Halcón reputation laid him open to grave personal danger at the hands of some mistaken peace officer or trigger-itchy professional gun-slinger out to get a reputation by downing El Halcón, and not above shooting in the back to acquire it, as Captain Jim had reminded him more than once. Slade would counter by pointing out that the deception opened avenues of information that would be closed to a known law enforcement officer, and that outlaws, thinking him just one of their own brand, sometimes got a mite careless, with disastrous results to themselves in consequence.

'Oh, all right, all right, go ahead your own loco Way!' Captain Jim would concede. 'Maybe you are right when you say that if your number ain't up, nobody can put it up! Go ahead!'

Which Slade would blithely proceed to do.

★ ★ ★

'Everybody 'pears to figure that pair of sidewinders gunned each other,' Orton remarked.

'Which is perfectly satisfactory with me,' Slade replied. 'I'm glad that nobody in the crowd paid any attention to details or they might have arrived at a different conclusion.'

'How's that?' asked the sheriff.

'Well,' Slade answered dryly, 'doesn't it seem a bit unusual that gents who did for each other would be lying side by side and both facing the same way?'

'By gosh, you're right!' exclaimed Orton. 'I never noticed it, and I'm purty sure nobody else did, either. Say, you don't miss anything, do you? Including what you shoot at.'

'Wouldn't have been wise to miss too many times tonight,' Slade said smilingly. The sheriff chuckled. Quickly, however, he was grave.

'I've a notion those hellions weren't riding for anybody hereabouts,' he remarked. 'I'm purty sure I would have recognized any of the boys who work for the neighborhood spreads.'

'Bill Weston did not recognize them, either,' Slade observed. 'Of course, though, they could have been recently hired. But if so, somebody will surely recognize them.'

For a moment, he was silent, then he abruptly arrived at a decision.

'You had them packed to your office?' he asked. 'That's right,' replied the sheriff. 'Got 'em laid out nice and comfy on the floor; the undertaker will pick 'em up in the morning. Didn't see any sense in routin' him out tonight.

Why'd you ask?'

'Because,' Slade said, rising to his feet, 'I'd like to take a look at them.'

'Okay,' agreed the sheriff. 'Just about three blocks to the office. Let's go.'

Curious glances followed them as they left the saloon together.

'Reckon some of the boys, who may have recognized you, are figuring I aim to lock you up,' chuckled Orton. 'Might be a good notion at that — would keep you out of trouble.'

53

It was but a short walk to the sheriff's office which was located in the squat courthouse building. They mounted a couple of steps and the sheriff seized the door knob and fumbled for a key. However, the door swung open as he turned the knob.

'Blast it! I was sure I'd locked that door,' he growled. 'Must be getting careless in my old age. Wait a minute till I strike a light.' He scratched a match and touched the flame to a bracket lamp. Light filled the room as he replaced the chimney. He glanced around, and swore an explosive oath.

'What the blankety-blank-blank!' he yelped, glaring in every direction.

The office was comfortably furnished with a table-desk and several chairs. This was all there was to be seen. The floor was otherwise cheerfully vacant.

Orton let out a bellow of wrath. He rushed to the desk, looked behind it, peered beneath it. Pounding across the room, he flung open a second door, struck another match and peered into a smaller room.

'They ain't here!' he howled.

Slade had already arrived at that conclusion, after a swift glance around. Although he was in no mood for mirth, he bit back a grin with difficulty. The sheriff's rage held a comical note.

'Cool down, and let's try to think this out,' he advised. 'You're sure you placed them in here, on the floor?'

'Am I sure!' yelled the scandalized peace officer. 'Of course I'm sure. I watched the boys lay 'em right there along-side the desk.'

'Well, they're not there now,' Slade said. 'And it's safe to say they didn't walk out, unless they were doing a remarkable chore of playin' possum.'

'But what does it mean?' demanded Orton.

'It means, I would say,' Slade replied dryly, 'that some body was extremely anxious for those bodies *not* to be placed on exhibition.'

'You mean they were riding for some spread hereabouts?' Orton asked.

'Possibly,' Slade conceded. 'If so, perhaps somebody will report a couple of hands missing.'

'I'll make some inquiries,' the sheriff promised. 'And you rule out the farmers as suspects?'

'Not altogether,' Slade disagreed. 'They wore rangeland clothes and, as I said, they did not handle their guns as one would expect farmers to do, but that is not conclusive. I do not think they were farmers, but I could be wrong, As the situation stands, anybody is suspect.'

'And sometimes folks hire gunslingers to do their fighting for them,' Orton observed shrewdly.

'Exactly,' Slade agreed. 'Which applies to both the ranchers and the farmers. And sometimes such characters get commpletely out of hand, as some reputable cattlemen learned to their cost. Incidentally, there is something you might do.'

'What's that?'

'Tomorrow, make a search of the various stables and hitchracks in town and learn if there are a couple of unclaimed horses hereabouts. If so, it might tell us something.' 'I'll do that,' nodded Orton. He began examining the door lock.

'Ain't busted, and I'll swear I turned the key in it when I left,' he announced.

'Quite likely you did,' Slade said. 'That old contraption would pose little difficulty to anyone with even a slight knowledge of locks, and we are getting specimens of late who know all the angles. Times are changing.'

'And for the worse, I'd say,' growled the sheriff. 'Looks like there ain't nothing safe anymore. Bustin' into the sheriff's office! Now what?'

'Now I think I could stand some more coffee,' Slade replied. 'We've done all we can here, having proved by ocular demonstration that there are no bodies present.'

'I reckon, whatever the devil that means,' grunted Orton. 'Okay, I'll lock the blasted thing again, though it looks like just a waste of time, Might as well leave the door open with a welcome sign hung out.'

Slade laughed and led the way to the outside.

When they reached The Widow Maker, Moore's place, he located a vacant table and sat down. The sheriff ordered a snort. Slade settled for coffee. Orton's still angry face relaxed in a grin.

'See some of the boys are lookin' a mite surprised,' he remarked. 'I told you they'd be figuring I was going to lock you up.'

'Perhaps they are just surprised to see you still in bad company,' Slade replied. Orton chuckled, and sampled his drink.

6

Sipping his coffee, Slade pondered the situation which, he felt, was interesting and rather ominous. He was still of the opinion that the two drygulchers were not farmers and never had been. Just as he was of the opinion that he himself had been their prime target. However, he was forced to admit that in both surmises he could be wrong. Weston was a talkative gent and had very likely been sounding off against the farmers in a manner that would arouse enmity. There was a bare possibility that the pair had been out to get Weston. Undoubtedly the first bullets fired had passed through the space Weston had occupied an instant before.

But Slade was decidedly inclined to discount that angle, as much as a Ranger discounted anything of which he was not sure; all angles must be explored.

He hoped he was right. Otherwise he was faced with the disagreeable intimation that a real range war was all set to erupt in violence. Which was disquieting, to put it mildly.

That, of course, was the obvious explanation of the things that had been happening in the section. But Slade had learned to view the obvious with suspicion. And he felt it did not explain in a satisfactory manner the various attempts to slow up the railroad construction. Those attempt had shown careful and shrewd planning and a knowledge of mechanics not usually associated with the average cowhand, And he was still pretty well convinced that the attempted drygulching was due to the fact that somebody had recognized him as *El Halcón* and considered it expedient to do away with him as quickly as possible.

Which meant, he believed, there was something afoot quite different from a routine row between cattlemen and farmers, productive of serious trouble though that could be. Something from which somebody hoped to reap an advantage and resented interference of the reputably *El Halcón* sort. What? To that he didn't have the answer, yet.

Well, after all he had been in the section but a few hours, not long enough to become really conversant with the situation as it stood. He must hold all judgment in abeyance until he had a chance to familiarize himself with conditions, and people.

Sheriff Orton finished his drink and glanced at the clock. 'I'm going to bed,' he announced. 'It's late and I'm likely to be plenty busy tomorrow night. How about you?'

'I think I'll follow your example very shortly,' Slade replied. 'Didn't have much sleep last night under a tree.'

'Where you sleepin' tonight?'

'Over at the railroad, in General Manager Dunn's private car,' Slade answered.

The sheriff shook his head. 'Going to risk that ride to night?' he asked.

'I don't think there is much risk,' Slade replied carelessly.

'I'll chance it.'

'Okay,' said Orton. 'See you tomorrow.'

He stalked out.

Bill Weston came over to join Slade. 'Everything all right?' he asked.

'Nothing to complain about,' the Ranger said. 'I'm going to bed.'

'Be here tomorrow, of course?' Weston stated rather than asked. Slade nodded.

'Then I'll be seeing you,' the cowboy promised. 'The boys and me are staying over for the trail herd bust — the Old Man said we could. Have another drink?'

Slade declined. 'Think I'll go to bed,' he repeated.

'Spect I will, too, after a couple more snorts with the boys,' Weston said cheerfully. Slade smiled as he watched him weave his way to the bar. He knew very well that Bill Weston would be right where he was till the last dog was dead.

Well, darn it! If he was just a carefree puncher with no thought for tomorrow, he'd be doing the same thing.

As it was, he waved goodnight to the owner and headed for the stable and Shadow.

He walked warily as he approached

the alley, although he had little fear of a repeat. In fact, he felt that whoever had staged the drygulching was not overly familiar with *El Halcón* and his ways of thinking and acting. Otherwise such a clumsy attempt would not have been made. Folks who were thoroughly conversant with *El Halcón's* methods realized that trying to drygulch him was just a watse of time with usually fatal results for the would-be drygulchers.

Although it was late, the stablekeeper was still up when Slade arrived, and regarded him with a curious look. 'You fellers must have been in the alley when the shootin' started,' he commented.

'We were,' Slade admitted. 'Know just what happened?'

'A couple of gents started throwing lead, and got themselves a case of lead poisoning,' Slade replied noncommittally.

'Uh-huh, so I gather,' was the keeper's dry response. 'I stayed right inside till things quieted down.'

'Always a wise thing to do,' Slade

conceded. 'Flying lead doesn't play favorites.' The keeper chuckled.

'Purty good way to put it,' he said. 'Well, hope you'll drop in again. Nice to have a gent like you, and a horse like that one.'

'Very likely I will,' Slade promised. 'Nice to know my horse is in good hands.' The keeper looked pleased.

'Be seeing you,' the Ranger said as he mounted and rode off.

The ride back to the railroad was without incident. After making sure his horse was properly cared for, *El Halcón* went to bed not to awaken until mid-morning.

The G.M.'s luxurious private coach boasted, among other things, a well-appointed bathroom, with plenty of hot water supplied by a locomotive boiler. So Slade enjoyed a thorough clean-up and a shave before sitting down to the breakfast Sam had ready for him.

'Boss man done gone out quite a while ago,' the colored man announced. 'Gone out with Mr. Becker.'

'Becker?'

'Uh-huh, Mr. Howard Becker, the engineer in charge. They done gone to look things over west of the town of Hamon. Don't know why; that town's supposed to be stoppin' point for this line. Survey lines already done been run to Hamon. That's why they're buildin' this big assembly yard and a shop and a roundhouse here, so they won't be clutterin' up the terminal. Never can tell what Boss man is up to, though. Always kickin' up some sort of bobberty. Man, oh man! Was I glad to see you ride up yesterday and put him back in a good temper. Ain't been fit to live with of late. He's all right this mornin', though. Mr. Slade, you sure got a way with you.'

'Thank you, Sam,' Slade replied, his cold eyes all kindness as they rested on the little old colored man. 'And Mr. Dunn is very fortunate to have you to fall back on when things don't go just right.'

'Mighty glad you feel that way about it, Mr. Slade,' Sam returned gratefully. 'Boss man sets a heap of store by what you think and say. When you gonna stop foolin' around and go to work for us, Mr. Slade? You'd mighty quick be a big man with the company. Wouldn't be surprised if you took over the Boss man's job when he gets too old to be bouncin' around.'

'I trust and hope it will be a long time before he stops bouncing around, Sam,' Slade said soberly.

'Amen to that, amen to that, Mr. Slade!' said Sam.

Slade was enjoying a cup of steaming coffee and a leisurely cigarette in the drawing room of the coach when Sam expclaimed, 'Here they come now! The Boss man and Mr. Becker.'

Slade glanced out the window as Dunn and his companion mounted the steps.

Howard Becker gave the impression of being a 'gray' man. His-hair was gray and so was his complexion, and there was, Slade thought, a gray quality to his thin-lipped smile as there was to his voice, which was toneless, a gray monotony, though pleasant enough. In build he was tall and lean with broad shoulders.

Dunn performed the introductions and Becker shook hands with a powerful grip.

In rather startling contrast to his otherwise grayness were his dark blue eyes that seemed to catch the light. Slade classified him as able and adroit and highly intelligent. All in all, the sort of man one would expect to be holding the re-sponsible and exacting position he did. He felt that Becker would do anything required of him with efficiency and dispatch.

Well, old Jaggers was noted for picking that sort, and he seldom made a mistake.

'I think I saw you in Lafe Moore's place last night, Mr. Slade,' Becker said. 'You did a good chore, setting that big cowhand back on his ears. He might have seriously injured that old Mexican with his loco horseplay.'

'How was that?' Dunn asked.

Becker told him, in the precise, detailed manner that could be expected of him. Dunn shook his head.

'Walt is always taking up for some

underdog,' he remarked.

'Heard there was a shooting — a double killing in town last night,' Becker observed.

'Understand there was,' Slade replied, letting it go at that. Later he would give Jaggers the details.

'Had your breakfast, Walt?' the G.M. asked. Slade nodded.

'Come on, Becker, and we'll have a bite,' Dunn told his companion. They moved into the little dining compartment. Slade finished his cigarette and went out to look things over. Very quickly be realized that Dunn's complaint that the sinister happenings slowed up the construction work was well founded. The workers were nervous and ill at ease. Some glanced slightly askance at the tall Ranger in his cowhand clothes. Undoubtedly any stranger so garbed was regarded with suspicion. Which was not strange.

However, he did manage to speak a few words with several foremen and from them garnered some information he considered of importance.

The assembly yard was, Slade thought, well laid out, attesting to Howard Becker's efficiency. As he strolled about he saw nothing to which exception could be taken. The rising machine shop and roundhouse were properly located. A couple of gravity humps, down which cars would roll under their own power to be switched onto various tracks, were of proper height and gradation. Everything should go smoothly and with dispatch were there no outside interference to get the workers jumpy.

Reaching the north limits of the yard, Slade leaned against a convenient tree, rolled a cigarette, and gazed toward the grim Tonto Hills to the north. They continued west for a long way, he knew, crossing the New Mexico state line. To the east, they petered out after a couple of miles, to be replaced by the level rangeland that extended far into the north and east. From them the Comanches, and those who came before the Indians, raided. Now wideloopers and other out-laws lurked in their canyons and gorges and launched sporadic forays against the prosperous cattle country and small settlements in both Texas and New Mexico.

And Slade knew it was not beyond the range of possibility that such gentry had something to do with the depredations committed against the railroad, the coming of which they resented.

Trouble between the cowmen and the farmers was, of course, their meat. With two armed camps concentrating on one another and each blaming the other for anything off color that happened, the outlaws had a free hand. An old owlhoot trick that worked.

However, *El Halcón* was not at all satisfied with such a comfortable conclusion relative to the recent assaults on the railroad. They had evinced an ingenuity that smacked of a carefully thought out campaign against the carrier and were foreign to the methods usually employed by cattle thieves and robbers.

All of which, Slade felt, gave him

plenty to think about and placed him in no position to risk snap judgments.

He turned and gazed south by west, and chuckled. A swarthy dust cloud was rising against the blue of the Texas sky, The kind of a cloud that billowed up from the steady plodding of many hoofs. The shipping herds were nearing Oresta. He looked forward to the coming night with anticipation and quickened pulses.

Oresta would soon be humming and he believed he was due a mite of diversion and a chance to briefly forget his problems. And often at such a time an opportunity of one sort or another might present itself. He strolled back to the private car in a carefree frame of mind.

7

Dunn and Becker had finished their snack and were out in the yard somewhere. So Slade again settled himself comfortably in the drawing room with a cigarette and coffee to await Dunn's return.

About an hour later, the old empire builder lumbered in and flopped into a chair.

'This ridin' all over heck and stumpin' around on cross ties is hard on old bones,' he said. 'Well, what do you think of Becker?'

'Appears to be very efficient,' Slade replied. 'He did an excellent chore on the yard.'

'Yep, he did,' Dunn agreed. 'A really good man. I'd like to keep him, but I doubt if he'll stay after this job is finished. He came to me highly recommended by a British firm United Machinery. He did work for them in Persia. I'm afraid,

72

though, that he's a world-wanderer, always on the go. After this line is finished, he's very apt to go gallivantin' off to some out-of-the-way corner of the earth.'

Slade nodded agreement. He was familiar with the type; just a variation of the chuck-line-riding cowhand or the boomer railroader. Always with an eye for fresh pastures.

'About that shooting in town last night Becker mentioned,' Dunn remarked. 'I've a notion you know more about that than you said. What did happen?'

Slade told him, in detail. Dunn swore with lurid vividness. 'So they're already after you, eh?'

'Looks sort of that way,' Slade conceded carelessly. Old Jaggers added a few more remarks that' smoked.

'Well, what do you think about it?' he asked.

'Nothing much, so far,' Slade answered. 'Too early to form anything like a definite opinion. Could have been some one with a grudge against *El Halcón*, although I hardly think so. And there is a remote possibility that they were really after Bill Weston. I really doubt that is true, but it's an angle that must not be dismissed without careful consideration. There is trouble between the cattlemen and farmers, that's true for certain, and I'm not prepared to make a guess as to just how serious it is or will become. All I can do at the moment is await developments, try to anticipate what's in the wind and, if possible, forestall it.'

'And you still don't think it's the cowmen who have been making the trouble for my railroad?'

'They may have been making some of it, like buzzing some slugs over the heads of a group of track layers, sliding the mules out of their corral and scattering them over the prairie. Those incidents and one or two more I learned about would be about their style. But certain other things, definitely not. 'For instance I learned that the outside rail on a curve was elevated enough to overturn a work train locomotive. That was a skillful piece of work and required certain technical knowledge one would certainly not expect from a bunch of cowhands. Same applies to the dynamitings, and boring brake cylinders, and filling journal boxes with emery dust.'

'The hellions could have hired somebody who knew how to do it,' Dunn suggested.

'Possible, but highly improbable, I'd say,' Slade answered. 'Well, we'll see. Perhaps I will be able to learn something in town tonight. Also, I hope to contact some of the owners and sound them out a bit.'

'And you also still think the blankety-blank M.K. bunch might be back of it all?'

'That was merely a surmise on my part,' Slade admitted. 'I'm not prepared to make a definite statement relative to that angle. I hope to be able to soon.'

'Okay, it's your baby,' Dunn said. 'You're going to ride to town?'

'Yes, very shortly,' Slade replied. 'Those shipping herds Sheriff Orton

75

mentioned should arrive before long and things should be lively.'

Slade did ride to town early, for he wished to contact Sheriff Orton and find out if he had learned anything in the course of the day. He found the sheriff in The Widow Maker, putting away a hefty surrounding.

'Got to lay a good foundation,' Orton explained. 'All heck is liable to be poppin' tonight. Instead of the three shipping herds we expected, five rolled in. Another hour or so and all those young hellions except the few that'll be standing night guard will be swarmin' all over town. Yep, it's liable to be quite a night.

'Nope, I didn't find any unclaimed horses,' he replied to Slade's question.

'Very likely whoever kidnapped the bodies from your office used them for transportation purposes,' Slade guessed. 'I'm of the notion they got them well away from town before disposing of them.'

'Expect you're right,' Orton agreed. He glanced toward the swinging doors.

'Here comes a shrewd article, and one I'm sorta keeping an eye on,' he announced.

The newcomer was a big man, tall and strongly built. He had a tight though well formed mouth, snapping black eyes, and a blocky face that was nevertheless, Slade thought, ruggedly good looking. His hair was black and inclined to curl. His bearing was assured and he walked with lithe grace despite his weight. His dress was that of a prosperous rancher and he wore a gun on the left side, butt to the front; evidently a cross-pull man. Slade wondered if he had mastered that difficult but extremely fast draw.

'Who and what is he?' the Ranger asked.

'Name's Dane, Jackson Dane,' the sheriff replied. 'Just what he is I ain't sure. He showed up here shortly before the farmers did. Had bought a big strip of land over to the west and to the north of their holdings. I've a notion the farmers would have liked to have that land, but Dane beat 'em to it.'

'Cattleman?'

'Darned if I know,' Orton admitted. 'Dresses like one, but he didn't bring any cows onto his holding. Didn't do any plowing, either. Built a nice ranch house and just sets there. Makes me wonder what the devil he has in mind.'

'Could be a promoter or speculator who saw opportunity to turn over a profit,' Slade responded, observing Dane who had passed to the far end of the bar and was conversing with Lafe Moore, the owner.

'In the nature of a mystery man, it would seem,' he remarked.

'Uh-huh, too darn mysterious,' grunted the sheriff. 'I don't like mysterious folks. My experience is that they'll stand watching.'

'And he bought land north of the farmers' holding, before they got title, I believe you said.'

'That's right,' replied Orton. 'Funny, the holding he bought runs way up into the hills, or so I heard. Why any body would want to pay out good money for those up ended hunks of rock is beyond me, but it seems he did buy it and pay for it. The hills are state land, too, of course. Reckon he got that chunk for next to nothing.'

'Very probably,' Slade agreed, his eyes thoughtful. 'Interesting, too.'

Just what he meant by that last remark he did not explain at the moment.

With a satisfied sigh, Sheriff Orton pushed back his empty plate and ordered a snort.

'Done swore in three special deputies,' he announced. 'With my three regulars, that gives me six good men to help me keep something like order. I've a prime notion I'll need them.'

El Halcón was of that opinion, also. Although it was just past sunset, The Widow Maker was already filling up with hands from the neighboring spreads and railroad builders. Soon, however, the more than a hundred cowboys from the five shipping herds that were bedded down on the outskirts of Oresta would come roaring in. Then business would really pick up. The owners of the various places were making preparations for the biggest night in quite a while. The dealers were at their tables, the bartenders were ready, the dance floor girls were coming on early. Slade felt his pulses quicken. After his long and lonely ride from Ranger post headquarters to the railhead, he had a desire for human companionship. He loved the rugged wastelands, wherein he found the maximum of content, but he was young, filled with lusty life, and there could be such a thing as a too extended period of peace and quiet with only his horse to commune with. Right now he was in the mood for Oresta's coming night of excitement and diversion.

Not that he could be altogether relaxed, for always in the back of his mind was the matter which brought him to the section, and he was continually on the lookout for anything that might bear on the problem that confronted him.

Being a Ranger was not all sunshine and roses and Texas bluebells; but there were recompenses that more than balanced the drawbacks. He chuckled to himself, ordered coffee and a sandwich, and listened with appreciation to the rising tumult inside and out.

Sheriff Orton drained his glass and placed it upside down on the table.

'Reckon I'd better mosey out for a look-see,' he said. 'You aim to stick around for a while?'

'For a while,' Slade replied. 'I'll see you later, here or elsewhere.'

With Orton's departure, Slade turned his attention to Jackson Dane, whom he had tentatively classified as a land promoter or speculator. Dane was still talking with Lafe Moore, the owner, in an animated way. Appeared the pair had a good deal to discuss.

He wondered why Dane had bought land he apparently intended to put to no use. Of course the coming of the railroad might have something to do with it. Which Dane had possibly learned was in the works long before the first survey stake was driven.

If so, he might have reasoned that with the added prosperity more adequate transportation would bring, the farmers might feel the need of more land for themselves or for others who desired to move into the section. In which case he might well be able to turn over his holding at a good profit. Not altogether unreasonable to believe so.

But why bad be bought into the hills, a terrain to all appearances worthless? Slade didn't have the answer, but the fact that Dane had bought a section of the hills interested him. The promoter, if such he really was, struck him as a man who didn't do something without a definite reason.

Well, it didn't matter and was no concern of his. It was just that his curiosity, which Slade felt was a failing with him, was excited. He dismissed Jackson Dane for the time being and turned his attention elsewhere.

Now the shipping herd hands were trickling in, gay, rollicksome, noisy young fellows for the most part, and The

Widow Maker was really beginning to boom. Slade leaned back comfortably in his chair and regarded the colorful scene. He decided he was thoroughly enjoying himself.

Gradually, however, being sensitive to such impressions, he felt that eyes were concentrating on him. Without moving his head, he let his glance slide along the bar to come to rest on Jackson Dane. The land promoter was gazing fixedly at him, a speculative expression on his rugged face. Slade wondered why he appeared so interested,

The explanation, however, was fairly obvious. Very likely Lafe Moore had been regaling Dane with an account of the happenings the night before, in which he, Slade, had played a prominent part.

Or perhaps somebody had whispered to him that the tall, black-haired man at the table was the notorious *El Halcón*. Slade bit back a grin as Dane, with a slight shake of his head, turned to Lafe Moore and said a few words. Once again he forgot all about Jackson Dane. There were more interesting things to contemplate, especially on the dance-floor. When he happened to glance toward the far end of the bar again, Dane was nowhere in sight. Evidently he had left the saloon. Slade once more focused his attention on the dance-floor. A little stepping with one of the girls wouldn't go bad. There were some lookers among them, all right, and he knew by the frequent smiles and glances cast in his direction he could just about take his pick.

While he was trying to decide which one to choose, a man came hurrying through the swinging doors. Just inside the doors he paused, searching the room with his eyes. His gaze centered and he weaved his way through the crowd to *El Halcón's* table.

'Mr. Slade?' he asked.

'That's right,' the Ranger replied.

The man held forth a nickel badge on which was engraved, 'Deputy Sheriff.'

'Mr. Slade, I'm Rader, one of Sheriff Orton's special deputies,' he announced. 'The sheriff told me to find you — said you would be here — and ask you to come to his office right away. He has something to show you, he said.'

'Okay,' Slade replied, rising to his feet. 'You coming along?'

The other, a rather scrubby looking individual, shook his head and grinned.

'I'm going to grab me a quick snort,' he said confidentially. 'Then, I'll have to hustle out on the street again. Orton told us to keep moving. Please don't tell him I stopped here to grab one.'

'I won't,' Slade promised. He had a feeling that Deputy Rader would very likely grab more than one before going back on duty. Well, that was his business.

8

Wondering what Orton had unearthed, Slade left the saloon and shoved his way through the jostling throng that crowded the main street. The courthouse sat on a side street that was much quieter. There were no other structures near it.

As he approached the building, he saw that a dim light burned in the sheriff's office. He mounted the steps, reached for the knob of the closed door. Then abruptly he drew his hand back and stood motionless, listening.

From inside the office had come a sound, a very faint but peculiar sound, barely audible. Anyone lacking *El Halcón's* marvelously keen hearing would almost certainly not have caught it. A queer, spasmodic thumping, as if somebody were lightly hammering a table with a gloved hand. It was an unusual sound, and Walt Slade had long ago learned to regard the unusual with suspicion. Just what was going on behind that closed door? For moments he stood straining his ears.

The sound persisted, never varying, except for an occasional soft scuttering, almost like a rat scampering back and forth with monotonous regularity. Something a rat was not likely to do.

In men who ride alone with danger as a constant stirrup companion there grows a subtle, seemingly inexplicable sixth sense that warns of peril when none apparently exists. In Walt Slade that sense was highly developed.

And now the voiceless monitor was setting up a clamor in his brain, something he never disregarded. Behind that closed door something was not right.

Standing well on one side, he reached out a cautious hand and gripped the door knob, exerted a barely perceptible pressure, and heard the bolt slide back. With a quick shove, he flung the door wide open.

There was a crashing boom. Buckshot howled through the opening. Slade went backward a half dozen steps, a gun in each hand, For a moment he stood motionless, the big Colts trained on the open door.

Nothing further happened. There was no sound except that spasmodic thumping that seemed to have taken on a frantic note. With the utmost caution he eased forward, cast a quick glance into the room, and looked squarely into the twin muzzles of a sawed-off shotgun.

★ ★ ★

Again he went backward, even though that one swift glance had told him the room was without human occupancy — the movement was instinctive.

The glance had also shown him the sawed-off was secured to the sheriff's desk so that the muzzles were trained on the door. A broken cord that passed around the butt dangled from the triggers. The other end of the cord had been tied to the door knob so that anybody trying to enter would have gotten the double charge dead center. An old trick with a brand new angle.

Without hesitation, Slade entered the office, guns ready for instant action nevertheless.

The door to the inner office was closed, and from beyond it came the frantic thumping, now much louder.

Passing across the room. Slade, again standing to one side, flung the door open. It struck against something with a muffled bump and swung back shut.

But now *El Halcón* understood. He opened the door again and shoved, not too hard. And as he did so, he saw that the something Which blocked its opening was the body of a man. The body of a man whose ankles were roped together, his arms tied behind him. In his mouth was a gag secured in place by a knotted handkerchief. His face was streaked with blood. It was his boot heels that had been spasmodically beating the floor.

Holstering his guns, Slade lifted him from beside the half open door and carried him to the outer office. He plucked the gag from his mouth and with a few swift slashes of his pocket knife freed his wrists and ankles.

'Who in blazes are you?' he demanded.

'I'm Bert Rader, one of Sheriff Orton's deputies' the other replied, his voice a hoarse croak.

And now Slade understood everything.

He lifted Rader to his feet and eased him into a chair. 'Take it easy and don't try to talk till I look you over,' he said.

Examination showed an ugly gash in Rader's scalp, just above the left ear. Slade probed the vicinity of the wound with his sensitive fingertips and concluded that there was no fracture and that the deputy was not badly hurt. He rolled a cigarette, lit it, and passed it to him. Rader puffed gratefully. 'And now,' Slade said, 'suppose you tell me what happened.'

'Orton left me in charge of the office,' Rader explained. 'A couple of fellers walked in and asked for the sheriff. I told them he was out somewhere. 'Is that him coming now?' one of 'em asked, pointing toward the window. I turned my bead and the sky fell in on me. Guess the other one belted me with a gun barrel or something.'

'Looks very much like he did,' Slade agreed. 'Go on.'

'It pretty well stunned me but didn't knock me clear out,' Rader continued. 'I sorta half asleep knew they were tying me up and gagging me and dragging me into the other office. Guess I just had sense enough not to make a noise. If I had, I reckon they would have come in and finished me.'

'They very likely would have,' Slade agreed. 'Here's another cigarette.'

'I could hear them doing something out here but didn't know what,' Rader resumed. 'Then I heard them shut the outer door and I began kicking the floor. I couldn't stand up, but I managed to roll over and over to the door and rub my shoulder against it and kept on kicking. Next thing the whole blasted place seemed to blow up-sure sounded that way. Then you shoved the door open and I saw you bending over me. What in blazes!'

His eyes, that had been vaguely staring straight ahead as he talked, suddenly rested on the shotgun clamped to the sheriff's desk.

'That's what you heard blow up,' Slade told him. 'Very fortunate for me that you were able to kick and make a noise; I heard it and got to wondering what was going on in here. Otherwise I would very likely have caught those blue whistlers dead center. Was a nice try, all right, but, thanks largely to you, it didn't work.'

Tersely he explained what preceded the attempt to blow him from under his hat. Rader clapped his hand to his shirt front.

'Yes, the blankety-blank took my badge!' he swore. 'My gun, too, of course. You're Mr. Slade, aren't you?'

'That's right,' the Ranger replied.

'Orton was telling me about you and how you larruped Hunch Meader.'

He broke off, eyeing Slade. 'And some

folks call you *El Halcón*, don't they?' he asked slowly.

'That's right,' Slade repeated, smiling slightly.

'Guess that sorta explains it,' said Rader. 'Some ornery sidewinders don't like you.'

'Right again,' Slade conceded, his smile broadening. Rader fingered his injured head and chuckled.

'Mighty glad I was able to do some kickin',' he said.

'Guess it pays to kick sometimes.'

'It certainly did in this instance,' Slade agreed heartily. 'At least from my viewpoint.' He walked to the door and peered out. 'Guess either nobody heard that scattergun let go or wasn't enough interested to investigate,' he remarked. 'At least nobody came around. Well, I reckon I'd better help you to the doctor to get patched up.'

'I'm just scratched,' Rader protested. 'There's some stuff in the desk drawer you can tie my noggin' up with and then, if you don't mind, I'd like to amble over to The Widow Maker for a snort or two. That'll do me more good than anything else. Orton said he'd be there later.'

Securing salve and a roll of bandage from the drawer, Slade deftly padded and bandaged the wound. Water and towels were available in the back room, with which he cleansed the deputy's face of blood.

'There, that should hold you for the time being,' he said. 'I don't think there is any evidence of concussion, but later you'd better have the doctor look at it, just in case.'

Rader stood up and grinned. 'Feller, you sure got a way with you,' he chuckled. 'I'm a new man. Head don't ache anymore; I'm rarin' to go.'

Slade ripped the shotgun from the desk and tossed it into the back room.

'Liable to scare the life out of anyone who happened to open the door,' he explained.

'A sorta new wrinkle, wasn't it?' observed Rader. Slade shook his head.

'No, it was not new,' he replied. 'I once

before encountered something similar. The way they set the trap was new, however, and very clever. The last place one would expect to run into such a contraption, the sheriff's office.'

'What I want to do most of all is line sights with that blankety-blank who stole my badge and posed as me,' Rader declared venomously. 'Think you'd know the sidewinder if you saw him again?'

'Yes, I'd know him if I saw him again,' Slade answered. 'But I doubt if I'll get a chance to see him. After he learns his little scheme failed I expect he'll trail his twine, pronto, and not show up around here for a spell. Let's go.'

As they stepped out the door, Rader chuckled again. 'Listen to the racket!' he said. 'No wonder nobody heard the gun go off. A wonder, too, that you heard me kickin' on the floor and rubbin' the door with my shoulder, through two closed doors. I couldn't get my feet up enough to hit the floor with my heels; I was just thumpin' with the soft counters of my boots and they didn't make much noise.'

'It was that queer muffled thumping and the slithering sound of you rubbing against the door that attracted my attention and caused me to start wondering just what the devil was going on inside,' Slade answered, not mentioning that the average pair of ears would not have heard the sound at all, much less classified it as a warning signal on the part of some otherwise helpless individual.

'Guess that's so,' Rader agreed. 'Say!- Looks like everybody from this end of Texas is in town tonight. There are some broncs with a SX burn. That holding is way over to the east and north.'

The principal streets were indeed jam-packed, and so were the saloons, and everybody appeared imbued with a single objective — to get drunk as quickly as possible. Slade also chuckled and his pulses quickened as he viewed the rowdy but colorful scene. The sense of irritation with which he had been inflicted because of being taken in so neatly by the pseudo deputy and coming so close to blundering into a trap was dissipating.

At the time his mind had been busy with other matters and it was not unreasonable to believe that the sheriff had really sent for him, conditions and circumstances being what they were. Oh, the devil! Nobody could always think of everything! And the scheme didn't work, which, after all, was the only thing that mattered. He shrugged his broad shoulders and threw himself into the spirit of the celebration.

Upon reaching The Widow Maker, they found Sheriff Orton at a table, looking expectant.

'Figured you'd be showing up soon,' he said to Slade. 'Sit down.' His eyes widened. 'Rader!' he exclaimed. 'What the devil happened to you? Why you got a rag tied around your head?'

Slade told him, in detail, stressing the part the deputy had played.

'Would appear that whoever cooked up the scheme was thoroughly familiar with your office and everybody connected with it,' he concluded. 'The hellion knew Rader's name, and he slipped away quickly after delivering his supposed message from you, very likely against the chance that somebody who knew otherwise might have heard him claim to be Rader.'

Sheriff Orton swore pungently and bellowed for a waiter. 'Snorts all around,' he told the one that came hurrying in response to that outraged roar and departed with equal speed under the sheriff's black glare.

'Poor jigger's wondering what he did wrong,' Slade chuckled, and smiled reassuringly at the waiter when he galloped up with the drinks.

'Everything's wrong!' growled Orton. 'Fill 'em up again as soon as they're empty,' he ordered.

'Yes, sir, yes, sir,' promised the waiter. 'I'll keep an eye on them, sir.'

It was Lafe Moore, the owner, who refilled the glasses from a bottle he brought to the table.

'Got to keep on the good side of the law tonight,' he said, crinkling his eyes at Slade. 'May need him.'

'You'll be lucky if you don't,' snorted

the sheriff. 'Blazes! What a night! And you ain't seen nothing yet. Just wait till the red-eye begins to really get in its licks. Much obliged, Lafe. Sit down and have one with us.'

Moore did so and gazed complacently around the crowded room. 'Noisy but behaving themselves pretty well,' he said. 'We get about the best characters here,' he observed to Slade. 'Mostly boys from the local spreads and lots of the railroad builders, who usually behave pretty well, too. Over to the west end of town it's a mite different. Most anything goes there and they get the rougher bunch.'

The sheriff nodded emphatically and drained his glass. 'Come on, Rader,' he said. 'We'll drop in on the doctor and let him patch you up, if you need more patching, Looks to me like Slade did a purty good chore on you. Come on, the doctor ain't going to bed tonight — figures on plenty of business. So long, Lafe. Be seeing you later, Walt.'

Together they worked their way to the door and departed.

'There comes Mr. Becker, the railroad man,' Moore suddenly announced. 'Nice quiet feller. Never has much to say, but what he does say is usually interesting. The big feller who was with me at the end of the bar, as Orton maybe told you, is Jackson Dane. He talks a lot but doesn't tell you anything much. He's a promoter or land speculator or some thing of the sort, I gather. I've a notion he figured to get in on the ground floor when he bought that stretch over to the west. The state lands were sorta wedge-shaped, wider up here to the north than farther south, and he's got a good holding. He knows this town is going to boom. Only a mater of time till all the shipping herds stop here to load. The old-timers are sorta slow to change, but they will change when they see the herds that are stopping here are underselling them. Wouldn't be surprised if Dane sells his land at a good profit.'

Slade had something of the same notion, but he was still puzzled about why Dane bought a stretch into the hills.

9

'Well, guess I'll have to be moving around,' Moore said. 'Have another drink.'

'I think I'll settle for a cup of coffee,' Slade replied. Moore beckoned a waiter and ambled off.

Howard Becker had found a place at the bar and was gazing moodily into his glass. If he had seen Slade, he gave no indication of the fact. He gave the impression, *El Halcón* thought, of a man who wished to be alone.

Well, that was his privilege and he very probably had plenty on his mind. His position with the railroad was an exacting one accompanied by no small number of problems. Sipping his coffee, Slade surveyed the room. As Moore said, the crowd was boisterous, noisy but fairly well behaved, with no indications of trouble starting. He wondered how things were in other places farther down the street. Doubtless quite different. He determined to go and see.

Might have the luck to encounter the fellow who posed as Rader, the deputy. Would be a pleasure to meet up with that gentleman. Pushing his empty cup aside, he left The Widow Maker.

The main street was still thronged with celebrants who were whooping it up for fair. Slade deftly wormed his way through the crowd that gradually thinned out as he drew farther west. But the saloons, if anything, became more frequent, dingier, and noisier. Here the lighting was not so good and the board sidewalk was broken in spots. There was, Slade felt, a general run-down air about this section of the town, which probably was shunned by the better class of citizens and visiting cowhands.

The kind of section, however, that was often favored by lusty young men who welcomed excitement, which very probably was to be found here without too much difficulty.

He paused before a place housed in a

rather dilapidated building but boasting a broad window much cleaner than most. He hesitated a moment, then pushed through the swinging doors. And got a surprise.

Despite its somewhat dubious exterior, the big room, crowded and noisy, was spick and span from its long gleaming bar to its equally gleaming dance-floor. Easing his way through the throng, he found a place at the bar and ordered a drink. A bartender in a white coat, spotlessly clean, served him, smiling pleasantly. He sipped the whiskey and found it good. Oh, well, you never could tell what you'd run into in a cow town.

A hand touched his elbow and he turned to glance down into a pair of very large and laughing blue eyes.

'Welcome to Gypsy's, Mr. Slade,' said a soft and nicely modulated voice.

Slade stared at the girl — young woman, rather. He figured her to be about twenty-two or three.

'You know my name,' he voiced the obvious.

'Of course,' she replied. 'Everybody knows *El Halcón*, the notorious outlaw.'

If he had been the sort to gasp, Slade would probably have gasped. The blue eyes laughed at him again.

'You are about all my cook has been talking about for the past thirty-six hours or so,' she said.

Your cook?'

'Yes, Miguel Allende, my cook. You rescued him from a bunch of cowhands who were having fun with him the other night. Bill Weston, the Boxed C range boss, learned Miguel was working for me — he's been with me only a little over a week — and came over to apologize and assure me Hunch Meader didn't really mean Miguel any harm. Then *he* started talking about you, and I couldn't shut him up.'

'You have my sympathy,' Slade smiled. I too have been bored by a similar discussion.'

'Didn't say I was bored,' she returned blithely. 'It was just that I couldn't get a word in edgewise and there were things I wished to ask Bill. According to him and Miguel, you are a veritable paragon of virtue despite your terrible reputation.'

El Halcón was by now feeling a trifle off-balance, but he managed to reply with a smile, '*Sans peur et sans reproche?*' 'That's it, 'Without fear and without reproach,' 'she instantly translated. Which didn't help to restore his equilibrium.

'You mentioned Miguel Allende, the Mexican, being your cook,' he remarked. 'Do you mean you own this place?'

'Yes, I own it,' she replied. 'I inherited it from my father a little over three years back.' She glanced around the room. 'Over by the corner of the dance-floor is a small table that isn't occupied at the moment,' she said. 'Perhaps we can reach it before somebody else grabs it, if you'd like to sit with me for a little while. I may have a question or two to ask *you*.'

'It will be a pleasure to answer any questions propounded by a charming lady,' he replied. She wrinkled her pert nose at him and led the way across the room. Slade's eyes followed her figure with appreciation.

She was small and slender, but with curves where curves were in order. Her curly hair was a smoldering reddish brown. He had already noted that her nose was slightly tip tilted with a few freckles powdering the bridge, her cheeks creamily tanned, her mouth red-lipped and nicely formed above a white round little chin that, he thought, bespoke determination.

They reached the table before somebody else occupied it.

She beckoned a waiter, who came hurrying, 'Drink?' she asked Slade.

'Coffee, if you don't mind,' he chose.

'Me, too,' she said. The waiter headed for the kitchen. 'And your name's Gypsy,' Slade said.

'Yes,' she answered, 'Gypsy Carvel.'

'Carvel?' he repeated. 'The owner of the Boxed C ranch is named Carvel, I believe.'

'That's right,' she said. 'He's my uncle. We don't get along too well. He and my father, who was his younger brother, didn't get along either. Especially after Dad came back from New Orleans with a wife and daughter and opened this place. My mother also is dead. When Dad died, Uncle Tom wished me to come and live with him at the ranch he's a widower and childless. He was scandalized when I insisted on staying here and running the place. I wanted to be independent and didn't see any reason why I shouldn't be allowed to run a saloon if I desired to. I've been doing all right.'

'You're not the first woman to run a cow town saloon,' he commented. 'I've known several who did, and made a go of it. An honest business when run properly.'

'That's the way I felt about it, and I run my place as it should be run, strictly on the level,' she said. 'But Uncle Tom couldn't see it. I'm sure that in his secret soul he's convinced that I'm headed straight for the devil with loose rein and busy spur.'

Slade laughed. Her manner of expressing herself was refreshing and amusing.

'You don't have any trouble?' he asked by way of making conversation while he studied her.

'Oh, some of the boys get a little rough now and then, but I have good floor men and waiters who quiet them down without much difficulty,' she replied carelessly, 'Nobody ever really has anything to complain of here. My dealers are square, and my dance-floor girls are nice, as you have doubt less already noticed.'

'I've been too occupied elsewhere to notice,' he answered meaningly.

The nose wrinkled again. 'Thanks for the compliment,' she said. 'Even a hoyden who runs a saloon likes to hear one now and then, even though she knows better than to believe it. Thank goodness here comes our coffee. I feel in the need of it about now — a busy night. And it's good to have an excuse to sit down for a little while.'

'Even with a notorious outlaw?' he bantered.

'Oh, I'm certain Uncle Tom believes

I'm one, or on the way to become one, which puts us in something of the same category,' she said.

'You mentioned that you might have a question to ask me,' he reminded her.

Instantly the big eyes were serious. 'Yes, I have,' she replied. 'A little while ago Uncle Tom was shot by somebody hidden in the brush. Mr. Slade, do you believe the farmers over to the west were responsible?'

'Frankly I do not,' Slade stated, without hesitation.

'Somehow I don't either,' she remarked thoughtfully. 'I have met some of them, and they certainly did not strike me as the kind of men who would do such a thing. Of course I haven't met all of them.'

'Nor have I,' he admitted. 'But I have associated with quite a number of their sort and always found that they ran pretty much to a pattern. Of course there is the possibility of a scalawag among them, but that I rather doubt. They cannot be pushed around, but they fight fair.'

'I'm glad to hear you say that, Mr. Slade,' she said. 'I would hate to see trouble between them and the cattlemen.' She hesitated a moment, then added, 'And somehow I have a feeling that you will keep that from happening.'

'Thank you,' he said. 'But why?' Again the moment of hesitation.

'When I was talking to Bill Weston,' she said slowly, 'I think he let something slip. In the course of enthusing over you, he mentioned that you saved his life. Then he shut up quickly and refused to explain. Won't you tell me what did happen?'

For a long moment Slade studied her before replying. 'Yes, strictly sub rosa,' he said and paused.

She did not immediately promise but regarded him in silence for a moment.

'You have an unusual way of expressing yourself, Mr. Slade, for — '

'An outlaw?' he prompted.

'You dress like a cowhand,' was her oblique reply. 'Very well, I'll counter with an expression I have heard the New

Orleans Creoles use, 'What the ears hear, the heart shall keep to itself alone.'

Slade told her of the drygulching in the alley. Her eyes seemed to darken and she shuddered.

'And those men were trying to kill you,' she said in the manner of one pronouncing a definite fact.

'Or perhaps Weston.'

She shook her head.

'No,' she said. 'Their intention was to kill *you*. Oh, Miguel told me much about you. Of how you are always helping others and making bitter enemies in consequence. They intended to kill *you*. Of course, though, Bill would also have been killed. They would not have left a witness.'

'You are probably right there,' Slade agreed soberly.

'I expect some of the Boxed C boys in any minute,' she observed. 'They nearly always show up when they are in town, to sort of keep an eye on me and make sure I'm okay, I've a notion.'

'In fact,' she added, 'I get quite a few

very nice people here now and then. There's Mr. Becker, the railroad man, whom you doubtless know, and Mr. Dane, the land speculator, as some call him. He's an affable sort, always cheerful. Mr. Becker is quiet and usually what I'd call somber, but very courteous.'

'Yes, he is,' Slade agreed. 'Mr. Dane is a good deal of a chatterbox, it would seem.'

'I think,' Gypsy began. 'Look! Here come Bill and Hunch now!'

The two Boxed C cowhands, undoubtedly somewhat the worse for wear, paused, glanced searchingly around the room and spotted Gypsy and Slade. Weston let out a joyous whoop and they came plowing to the table.

'Well, if this ain't fine!' boomed Weston. 'So you two got together! What'd I tell you, Gyp, ain't he all I claimed for him?'

Gypsy's eyes met Slade's squarely. 'Yes,' she replied, 'and more.'

Weston chortled gleefully. 'Yep, this is fine,' he repeated. 'Come on, Hunch, let's have a snort to celebrate!'

They weaved their way to the bar, near the swinging doors, and hammered for service.

'They're impossible, but nice, when you get to know them' Gypsy said. 'But really, Mr. Slade, I'll have to leave you for a while. I see my head bartender looking this way. I think he wants something. I'll see you a little later. Don't go out, now.'

'I won't, Miss Carvel,' he promised.

'Never mind the Miss Carvel,' she retorted. 'Everybody calls me Gypsy.'

'And people who like me usually call me Walt,' he returned pointedly.

Again the big eyes met his. 'All right — Walt,' she said softly. 'Go over and have a drink with the boys, now, on the house. It will please them.'

With which she whisked away through the crowd to the far end of the bar. Slade's eyes followed her progress, again with appreciation. Chuckling, he got up and strolled toward where Weston and Hunch were standing.

He was directly opposite the door when three men bulged in. Slade recognized the foremost as the scrubby individual who had posed as Deputy Rader.

The recognition was instantly mutual. The fellow gave a yelp of fright, surged back against the others, and jerked a gun. Slade drew and shot him before he could line sights. His dying hand squeezed the trigger and the bullet slashed the floor at Slade's feet. His companions fired over his sagging body, whirled and fled. One slug grazed Slade's forehead and sent blood pouring into his eyes, half blinding him. He fired three swift shots at the general direction of the door. But now the Boxed C hands were in action. Roaring profanity, big Hunch charged forward, hurling men right and left, and nearly took the swinging doors from their hinges as he tore through them. Slade heard him blazing away outside and hoped he wouldn't kill an innocent pedestrian.

His fears were allayed somewhat a moment later, however, as Hunch came bellowing in again. Slade dashed the blood from his eyes, holstered his guns and began wiping his face with a hand-kerchief.

'They got away!' bawled Hunch, waving a cocked gun in the direction of the wildly scattering crowd. 'They tried to kill Walt! Anyhow, you did for one of the skunks,' he told *El Halcón*. 'Got him dead center, the blankety-blank-blank!'

Gypsy was beside Slade. 'You're hurt!' she exclaimed, her eyes wide with anxiety. 'Come along to the back room so I can look you over.'

'Just a scratch,' he deprecated the injury, which really was very slight.

'I'll be the judge of that,' she retorted firmly. 'Come along!' She seized his arm and dragged him after her, Weston and Hunch clearing a path for them.

'Find the sheriff,' she called to a floor man in passing.

In the back room, Hunch slammed the door shut. Gypsy forced Slade into a chair.

'Water and a clean towel,' she told Weston, who charged out again to return a moment later with what she ordered.

She resolutely went to work on *El Halcón*, who was becoming mildly amused by the whole episode.

He experienced a feeling of satisfaction, too; he had evened the score with the horned toad who tried to shotgun-blast him. He relaxed in the chair and let her have her way.

Her little hands were deft and efficient. Very quickly she had the bleeding stopped and the slight wound padded and bandaged.

'I've had a lot of experience with such things during the past three years. It's become second nature to me,' she said. 'Always somebody getting *scratched*, as you call it. There, that should hold you. I don't think I did a bad job.'

'It was wonderful,' he replied. 'I'm going out and get shot again.'

'Don't you do it, the next one might be beyond me,' she warned. 'Why did that man try to kill you, Walt?'

Knowing that the story was bound to get around sooner or later and feeling it was better for her to have a first-hand account, Slade regaled his absorbed listeners with a review of the contraption rigged up in the sheriff's office, the attempt that failed.

'And the other two sidewinders got away! Why can't I ever learn to hit what I aim at!' wailed Hunch.

'You'd do better if you aimed at somebody else, then you might plug the jigger you want to,' Weston commented. 'Here comes the sheriff.'

Orton hurried in, looking apprehensive. 'You all right?' he asked Slade,

'I'm being pampered,' the Ranger replied cheerfully. 'You can stand some,' snorted the sheriff. 'Anyhow you're in good hands. Figure he's okay, Gyp?'

'Yes, he'll make out,' Gypsy replied. 'This time, at least,' she added, her eyes somber.

Slade stood up. 'Let's take a look at that hellion,' he suggested. He and the sheriff left the room together.

'You figure he ain't hurt much, Gyp?' Weston inquired anxiously.

'Very little, thank Heaven,' Gypsy

replied, and added, 'but I've a notion that before all is said and done, I'll very likely succeed in getting hurt a good deal more.'

Weston looked puzzled, but she did not explain what she meant by that.

10

Outside the room, Slade and the sheriff examined the dead man, a very ordinary looking individual nobody could recall seeing. His pockets revealed nothing of significance save a good deal of money which the sheriff confiscated.

'Will help pay for planting him,' he remarked. 'A sort of narrow escape for you, though, wasn't it?' he remarked to Slade.

'It was,' the Ranger conceded. 'He very nearly caught me off balance. Caught him off balance a mite, too, I imagine; he looked like he was seeing a ghost. Quite likely he hadn't learned that his shotgun scheme didn't work. Otherwise, I've a notion he would have hightailed out of town.'

'Well, he hightailed out, all right,' grunted Orton, 'and I figure he ain't coming back. A pity the others got away. I gather Hunch came very near to killing a few folks who weren't in on the deal.'

'Contrary to general opinion, few cowhands are good shots,' Slade remarked. 'And I fear Hunch comes into that category.'

'He couldn't hit a barn if he was locked inside of it,' Orton growled. 'Now what?'

'Now I think I'll have a little more coffee,' Slade said. 'I see the waiter is holding my table.'

'A good notion after losing blood,' agreed the sheriff.

'I'll have some with you.'

However, it was not the waiter but Gypsy Carvel herself who brought the coffee, and then joined them in a cup. The place had been in a good deal of an uproar after the shooting, but had quickly quieted down as the patrons went back to the serious business of drinking, poker playing and dancing with the girls.

'A wild night everywhere,' remarked Orton. 'A lot better here than in most places. I expect another killing or two be fore the last dog is dead. This is one of the biggest nights Oresta has ever known."

'We'll go out and look things over,' Slade said.

'And please try to keep out of trouble,' Gypsy begged as she pushed back her empty cup and prepared to return to her chores.

'I will, if you'll promise to do the same,' Slade replied, his eyes laughing at her.

'I won't,' she declared flatly, and was gone.

'Now what the devil did she mean by that?' wondered the sheriff.

If Slade knew, he didn't see fit to explain.

A couple of the special deputies, rounded up to pack the body to the sheriff's office, trudged off with it on a shutter. 'I sent word for 'em even before I knew for sure what had happened,' Orton said, 'Knew darn well they would be needed. Ready to go?'

Slade was and they left the saloon together, Gypsy Carvel's eyes following them through the swinging doors.

'She's all right,' Orton remarked, apropos of Gypsy. 'She and old Tom had quite a row when she decided to run the place, after her dad died. I know darn well he has a soft spot in his heart for her and worries because she's in a business he figures she oughtn't to be. He wanted her to come and live at the ranch with him — said that was where she belonged — but Gyp couldn't see it that way. She hankered to be independent, and she is.'

'She belongs to a different generation,' Slade said. 'A generation in which the status of women is swiftly changing. They are entering the business world — in one way or another, and some of them are already displacing men. Take old Hetty Green, for example. She is called the wealthiest woman in America, and the chances are she is. She inherited a very moderate fortune but by her shrewdness and initiative she's achieved enormous riches. There is scarcely a large-scale in-dustrial enterprise in which she is not represented, and she has big real estate holdings in New York and Chicago, and makes the Wall Street tycoons sit up and take notice. Women are no longer utterly dependent on men, economically speaking. Gypsy will do all right and the chances are that sooner or later Old Tom will come around to her point of view.'

'Expect you're right,' Orton agreed. 'He holds his comb pretty high but he's liable to end up getting it clipped.'

Sheriff Orton had not exaggerated when he said it was a wild night. Although it was long past midnight, the streets were still thick with people most of whom, it appeared, had achieved their ambition to get drunk and who were filled with a burning desire to make as much noise as possible.

The scene, Slade thought, was in a way atavistic, livid, medieval. A dance of Apaches on the war-path, a dance of vampires under a voodoo moon, a dance of nymphs and satyrs. For now there were women on the streets. Girls who had drifted from the dance-floors with male companions were adding their shrill laughter to the tumult. Song, or what was apparently meant for it, bellowed over the swinging doors, and mingled with the cheerful clang of gold pieces on the mahogany, the clink of bottle necks on glass rims, the thumping of boots, the clicking of high heels, shouts, curses, and the incessant gabble of voices. Oresta's uproar rose stridently to the shuddering stars.

'And what in blazes are you going to do about it?' growled the sheriff. 'There are around two hundred cowhands in town tonight, most of them young hellions full of the devil. And about as many rock busters from the railroad. The blasted railroad *would* have to pay off today! If I had fifty deputies on the job they couldn't quiet 'em down.' Oh, well, it's happened before and it will happen again,' Slade answered. 'And usually no great harm is done.'

He was right, in this particular instance, at least. The sheriff's earlier gloomy prediction was not realized. There were some cuttings, some busted heads and bloody noses, but nobody got killed. The shotgun-rigging outlaw was the sole casualty, and he wasn't missed.

124

And as the hours dragged toward the rose and gold of the dawn, the din lessened. Tired nature was taking toll; for after all, most of the revellers had worked hard all day, and there would be more work to do on the morrow. Slade glanced at his watch.

'I think I'll call it a night,' he announced. 'I don't think there's much use in sticking around longer — nothing more to learn, so far as I can see. Guess I'll grab Shadow and high tail.'

'I don't like to think of you taking that lonely ride tonight, the way things are,' the sheriff worried. 'Those other two sidewinders may be around somewhere, and the devil only knows what they might cook up.'

'Well, I've got to sleep somewhere,' Slade pointed out."And there's sure no place here tonight.'

'Wait!' exclaimed Orton in the voice of one who is in spired. 'I got a notion. Come on, we're going back to Gypsy's place.'

When they arrived at the saloon, the

crowd there had pretty well thinned out and the barkeeps and floormen were making suggestive remarks to the die-hards.

Gypsy was at a table with a cup of coffee for company.

Orton led the way to her.

'Gyp,' he said, 'don't you have a couple of rooms up stairs, beside yours, that you now and then rent out to some of the Boxed C boys?'

'That's right,' Gypsy replied. 'Why?'

'Because,' the sheriff explained, 'I don't like the notion of Slade riding back to the railroad by himself tonight. I was wondering if you could put him up for the night Don't you figure it's a good idea?'

'A darn good idea,' Gypsy agreed. Her eyes met Slade's and suddenly she blushed and lowered her lashes.

'I'll take care of it right away,' she said hurriedly and headed for the back room, from which a staircase led to the second story of the building.

Slade glanced at Sheriff Orton. That old schemer wore a very pleased expression.

11

When Slade arrived at the railroad, shortly after noon, he found Jaggers Dunn in a cheerful frame of mind.

'Nothing bad happened last night, so far as I know,' the G.M. explained, 'Some of the boys showed up from their hell raising with marks of conflict, but none of 'em were disabled. How was it with you? What happened to your head?' he added, peering at the strips of plaster that had replaced Gypsy's bandage. Slade told him, starting at the beginning with the incident of the rigged shotgun. Dunn said quite a few things that wouldn't sound well at a board of directors' meeting.

'The hellions are after you hot and heavy, eh?' he growled. 'What's to do about it?'

'Nothing, except await developments,' Slade answered. 'I'm still not sure why they want me, whether it's my

El Halcón reputation getting a work-out, or something else. I'm inclined to believe something else.'

'What?' Dunn asked.

'That question remains,' Slade replied. 'I'm still endeavoring to find the answer.'

'And you still think the M.K. bunch might be back of the things that have happened?'

'It is an angle that must be considered,' Slade said. 'I'm going to do a little browsing around and see if I can find the answer to a couple of things that puzzle me. I'll have a cup of coffee with you and then I'm going to take a little ride.' After drinking his coffee and chatting a while with Dunn, Slade rode west at a good pace. For a while he rode parallel to the railroad line and not far from the right-of-way. On and on stretched the shining steel ribbons. But Slade knew they did not stretch nearly as far as Jaggers Dunn had hoped they would by this time. They still had some nine miles to go before reaching the supposed-to-be railhead at Hamon, the farmers' town.

A material train rumbled past, the locomotive's stack booming, side rods clanking. A derisive whistle blast sounded.

Slade smiled slightly, for he knew suspicious eyes were peering from engine cab and caboose. He watched the bobbing rear markers dwindle in the distance.

Now he was noting clumps of cattle that bore the Boxed C burn; he was passing over old Tom Carvel's holding. A little later, after a searching glance around the prairie, he turned north toward the rugged Tonto Hills, veering slightly to the west. Another hour and he was approaching the brush-grown lower slopes.

And now he became more alert. No telling what that chaparral might hide, although he hardly expected to contact anything of an inimical nature. Best not to take chances, however, after his recent experiences.

After a bit he turned due west and rode along parallel to the base of the slopes. Another hour and, estimating the distance he had covered, he knew he must be beyond the eastern edge of Jackson Dane's holding, what was formerly state land. The range was still excellent but he saw no more cattle. Evidently the Boxed C hands kept their charges off Dane's land. He moved a little closer to the slopes, studying them with care.

A mile farther on and he sighted the shadowy mouth of a narrow, rock-walled canyon. Pulling Shadow to a halt, he sat for some minutes sweeping the prairie with his eyes; there was nobody within the range of his keen vision. He spoke to Shadow and entered the canyon.

Now he slowed the big black to a walk and his gaze roved over the rocky wall. He was perhaps a mile up the canyon, which appeared to extend for an indefinite distance, when he approached a little spring that seeped from beneath the cliff. He turned Shadow toward it and the horse thrust his muzzle into the water, took a swallow, raised his head with a displeased snort, and shook a shower of glittering drops from his muzzle.

Slade dismounted, scooped up a little

of the water in his palm, and touched his lips to it. It was clear and cold but had a slightly bitter, astringent taste.

'It won't hurt you,' he told Shadow, 'but I've a notion you don't particularly care for the taste of it. Can't say as I blame you.'

Straightening up, he studied the cliff face, his gaze travelling across its beetling surface to center on a faint greenish tinge a score or so of feet above the ground.

'May be vegetation stain, but I don't think so,' he remarked to the horse. 'Feller, I'm beginning to get a notion about something. Let's see what else we can find. Maybe a better snort for you.'

He mounted and continued his slow ride up the canyon. Twice again he noted the greenish stain that intrigued him. A little later he spotted a second spring, on the far side of the canyon, from which Shadow drank his fill.

'Tastes different, eh?' his master remarked. 'Just as was to be expected. Bet you the next one, over on the other side, will be one you won't like the savor of.'

Which proved to be the case. And nearby was yet another greenish stain on the cliff face, very faint but discernible to Slade's unusually keen vision.

'Yes, horse, I believe we have hit it,' he said as he turned Shadow's nose down-canyon. 'A very simple explanation of something that has puzzled some folks, including our worthy sheriff. And myself, for that matter, for a while, although I had begun to suspect something of the sort. Okay, horse, let's head for home. Be long past dark by the time we get there, but I consider our little jaunt paid off. We can discount one angle at least.'

The sunset was flaming its scarlet and gold splendor in the west as he rode across Tom Carvel's land — the old rancher's *casa* was some miles to the south, he had gathered from Sheriff Orton — and the stars were blossoming their silver beauty before the lights of Oresta came into view. He did not pause at the railroad yards but continued to town.

After making sure all Shadow's wants were properly cared for, he repaired to Gypsy Carvel's place for something to eat. He found a vacant table and sat down. A floor man hurried to the back room and Gypsy appeared at once.

She was subtly changed from the day before. Her eyes were downcast, her cheeks rosier than even was their wont, her voice soft and low when she greeted him.

'I hoped so hard you'd be back tonight that I insisted to myself that you would and waited to eat with you,' she said. 'And, dear, Miguel has fixed something extra special for you; said he feels like celebrating.'

'I don't suppose you had a hand in that,' Slade remarked, innocently, his eyes laughing at her.

'Well, I did help a little,' she admitted demurely, her red lips wreathing an answering smile. 'Sheriff Orton was in a while ago, said he would be back. He looked so smug and satisfied; he's too darned observant!'

133

'He was inspired, and very under-standing, don't you think so?' Slade said. Gypsy blushed and without replying hurried to the kitchen.

A little later she reappeared, leading two waiters who bore Miguel's elaborate preparation, the old cook beaming after them from the kitchen door.

'How's this?' Gypsy asked.

Wonderful!' Slade enthused. 'Almost as wonderful as — '

'Will you please shut up and eat your dinner!' she interrupted.

'I fear that would be a complicated process,' he grinned. 'But perhaps I can manage it.'

Before eating, Slade walked to the kitchen door and thanked Miguel for his thoughtfulness.

'It is a pleasure,' the old man mur-mured. 'The very great pleasure to serve *El Halcón*. And,' he added, 'his charming *señiorita*.'

'Miguel,' Slade chuckled, 'your taste in women is as good as your taste in food.'

'*Capitán*, I, too, was young once, long

ago,' Miguel replied, loud enough for Gypsy, who was approaching, to hear.

'Miguel? Back inside with you,' she ordered. 'You're as bad as he is.'

Miguel departed, grinning. Gypsy made a face at his retreating back.

There was worse to come.

While they were eating, Sheriff Orton entered, bought a drink at the bar, and strolled to the table, smiling benignly.

'Well! Well!' he chuckled. 'What a scene of domestic tranquillity.' He raised his glass. 'Here's to the —'

'Don't you say it!' Gypsy stormed at him. 'Uncle Brad, you're impossible! Sit down and I'll share my dinner with you.'

The sheriff drank his incompleted toast and sat down.

They had a very pleasant dinner together, after which Gypsy trotted off to her chores. The sheriff turned expectantly to Slade.

'Well, learn anything today?' he asked.

'Not a great deal,' the Ranger replied. 'Cleared up a supposed-to-be mystery, confirming what I had already begun to

135

expect, and eliminated a barely possible suspect. Tell you about that later. Otherwise, I feel I accomplished nothing. I still haven't the slightest notion who is back of the heck raising hereabouts, and am not at all sure why. Altogether I seem to be getting exactly nowhere.'

'I figure you're not doing too bad,' the sheriff said, 'At least, you managed to rid the earth of three pests, which is something.'

'But not enough,' *El Halcón* said. 'Just some hired hands who bungled their chore. May put the big jigger, whoever he is, in a bad temper, though, and possibly cause him to do something foolish.'

'Sure looks like somebody is mighty het up about your presence in the section,' observed Orton. 'I've a notion you're giving the sidewinder a case of the jitters. For if he really knows something about you, he also must know it's no joke to have *El Halcón* on your trail.'

'Possibly,' Slade conceded, with a smile. 'Up to the present, however, whoever he is has been mostly on my trail. He's kept me stepping pretty lively to stay alive. Of course he has an advantage, at the present; he knows whom to look for while I don't.'

'Won't last,' the sheriff declared positively. 'You'll have him on the run before all is finished. And the chances are he won't be able to run fast enough. And that ain't guess work, it's based on past performance.'

'Hope you're right,' Slade said cheerfully. 'Well, we'll see. How about another snort?'

'Don't mind if I do,' the sheriff accepted. 'Having one with me?'

'If you don't mind, I think I'll settle for another cup of coffee,' Slade said.

'You and your coffee!' snorted Orton. 'No wonder you and Gyp get along so well; that's all she ever drinks, so far as I've been able to see.'

'To which her complexion attests,' Slade smiled.

'Ain't nothing wrong with my complexion,' declared the sheriff, vigorously rubbing a wrinkled cheek, 'and I hardly ever touch the darn stuff. Straight likker is a man's drink and keeps him on his toes. Everybody to his taste, though, as the herder said when he kissed the sheep. Oh, by the way, I expect old Tom Carvel in town tonight — chances are he's already here. He'll be at The Widow Maker. Drop in there after a bit, I'd like to have you meet him.'

'I'll do that,' Slade promised. 'I also would like to meet him.'

The sheriff chuckled. 'Tell you something funny about the old coot,' he said confidentially, glancing around and lowering his voice. 'Whenever he is in town he moseys down this way.'

'He comes in here?'

The sheriff shook his head. 'Nope, he never comes in. He just waits till well after dark, when there ain't nobody much on the street down here, except on paydays or a bust night like last night, and then he eases out of The Widow Maker and ambles off, looks back, turns a corner and heads for this street. He slows up when he gets close to Gyp's place and peeks in the window. Wants to look at her to see she's all right. I caught onto it by accident and I never let on. As I told you before, he's got a soft spot in his heart for her, despite all his big talk and pawin' sod. A pity they can't get together again.'

'Yes, it is,' Slade agreed thoughtfully. 'She looked worried when she mentioned to me that he was shot and wondered if the farmers were responsible. I've a notion she has a soft spot in *her* heart for *him*.'

'I wouldn't be surprised,' Orton conceded. 'Women are funny that way — they can't get along with a man but may like him a lot just the same.'

'Come to think of it,' Slade remarked, 'do you intend to hold an inquest on that fellow who was killed here last night?'

The sheriff shrugged. 'Coroner is out of town; don't know when he'll be back. I didn't think the hellion would keep so I had him planted today. What's the sense of holdin' an inquest? Everybody knows how he was killed and that he had it coming. Would be just a waste of time.'

Slade smiled and let the subject drop. Such unorthodox procedures, he knew, were not uncommon in cattle country.

Orton glanced at the clock, shoved his empty glass aside. 'Guess I'd better mosey out for a look around,' he announced. 'You say you'll be at The Widow Maker later?'

'Yes, after a while,' Slade replied.

'Okay, I'll see you there,' the sheriff promised and took his departure. Slade settled comfortably in his chair for a cigarette and waited for Gypsy to return, which she did before long.

'Quiet tonight,' she said, glancing around. 'To be expected, though. I imagine most of the boys are recuperating after last night.'

It was Slade's turn to glance at the clock. 'I'm going up to Lafe Moore's place for a little while,' he told her. 'I'll be back shortly.'

'Please do,' she said. 'I expect we'll close early tonight.'

140

'Yes?'

She met his laughing gaze and blushed. 'Yes,' she said softly.

12

Outside the saloon, 'Slade strolled along the rather gloomy street. He had covered but a few blocks when he saw a man walking toward him from the other direction. As he passed beneath a street light, Slade saw that he was elderly and wore the garb of a prosperous rancher.

As usual, *El Halcón* was walking close to the building walls and taking careful note of his surroundings. Between him and the approaching rancher was a dark alley mouth which the other pedestrian would reach first did he hold his present pace. Alley mouths, especially those opening onto a shadowy and practically deserted street, always held *El Halcón's* attention. He was but a few yards distant, shouldering the building wall, when the other reached it.

From the shadows bulged two men. Slade's keen eyes caught a glimpse of metal as one swung a blow at the old man's head. The rancher's hat flew off and he fell.

Slade bounded forward. The man who struck the rancher whirled to face him. Again Slade caught the gleam of shifted metal as a gun muzzle lined toward him. He drew and shot, and again.

The gun wielder pitched forward with a coughing grunt. His companion darted into the alley, Slade speeding him on his way with a couple' of slugs.

Gliding forward, a glance told the Ranger there was nothing to fear from the attacker on the ground. He peered cautiously into the alley and caught a glimpse of the fugitive just rounding the corner at the far end of the lane.

The oldster was snorting and swearing and struggling to rise. Slade helped him to his feet and saw he was bleeding from a gash just above his left temple. However, the vigor of his profanity indicated, the Ranger thought, that he was not seriously injured.

'Take it easy, sir,' Slade told him. 'Let me take a look at your head.'

'Okay, son,' the oldster growled. 'Don't think it amounts to much, but if it hadn't been for you, the chances are I'd have got a hell of a sight worse. Those blankety blank nesters!' A swift examination led Slade to conclude that the injury was not serious but needed attention. Heads were poking cautiously from the doorways of saloons further up the street, but nobody approached. Evidently it was not considered good manners in this section to horn into fights. Nor good judgmment, either.

'Just a minute, sir, and I'll take you to where you will be patched up,' he told the other. He turned the dead man over on his back and peered into his face. With a mutter of satisfaction, he recognized him as one of the pair that accompanied the shotgun-rigger into Gypsy Carvel's saloon and escaped big Hunch's barrage of poorly aimed lead.

He considered this significant and it gave him a very good notion as to the identity of the man he had rescued. He retrieved the fallen hat and returned it to its owner, who jammed it on his head, swore as it pressed on the cut, and shoved it farther back. He fixed Slade with a pair of intolerant blue eyes.

'Son,' he said, 'I'm mighty beholden to you, and I won't forget it. If Tom Carvel can ever do you a favor, don't be slow in asking.'

'Thank you, Mr. Carvel,' Slade replied, biting back a grin and highly pleased at the way things were working out.

Old Tom was measuring his more than six feet of broad-shouldered height with his shrewd old eyes.

'Say!' he suddenly exploded, 'I betcha you're the young feller Bill Weston and my boys were soundin' off about! Slade the name?'

'That's right,' the Ranger admitted. Old Tom thrust out a gnarled paw.

'Shake!' he said. 'You're quite a feller.'

'Thank you again, sir,' Slade said as they shook with vigor.

'Come along now, sir.'

Taking Carvel's arm he propelled him along the street.

Glancing over his shoulder he saw that men were cautiously approaching the body. Let them do a little guessing.

They reached Gypsy's place and Slade turned his charge toward the door. Carvel hung back.

'Say!' he exclaimed, 'I don't go in there.'

'Mr. Carvel,' Slade reminded him, 'a little while ago you said that if you could ever do me a favor, I was not to hesitate requesting it. Well, I'm requesting one right now — that you'll go right in with me. Incidentally, Gypsy will be very, very glad to see you.'

Old Tom grunted and swore but Slade gently but firmly steered him through the swinging doors.

Gypsy was at the table where he had left her, waiting. She stared, gave a startled cry, sprang to her feet and ran to them. 'Uncle Tom!' she exclaimed. 'Oh, what happened to you? You're all bloody.'

'Gyp, I didn't mean to come in,' old Tom muttered shame facedly. 'He made me.'

146

'He makes everybody do just what he wants them to,' Gypsy replied. 'But you're hurt!'

'It's not serious,' Slade hastened to reassure her. 'He just met with a small accident.'

'But it wouldn't have been small if it hadn't been for him,' Carvel declared emphatically, 'The blasted nesters would have done me in sure as shooting.'

'Mr, Carvel,' Slade said quietly, 'I don't think those men were farmers. I'll explain why later. Now into the back room with you and let your niece patch you up. She's good at that; did a bang-up chore on me last night. Didn't you, Gypsy?' he added.

'I'm glad you think so, dear,' she said, blushing and smiling. 'Come along, Uncle Tom. Nothing is gained by arguing with him.'

While Gypsy deftly treated her uncle's injury, Slade pondered how things unexpectedly worked out. Coincidence? No. The only element of coincidence was in that he had left the saloon when he did

147

and not a few minutes later. Very probably others beside Sheriff Orton had noted that Carvel made his pilgrimage to the west end of town whenever he happened to be in Oresta. In Slade's opinion, the attack on the rancher had been planned. For he was firmly convinced that the two devils who staged the attack were members of the mysterious outfit that was deliberately stirring up trouble in the section. The killing or serious injury of Tom Carvel would have greatly heightened the friction between the cattlemen and the farmers. 'There, that'll hold you,' Gypsy said, giving the bandage a final pat and stepping back.

'Send somebody to The Widow Maker to tell the sheriff to hustle down here,' Slade said.

'And have him tell Bill Weston I'm here okay and will be seeing him shortly,' old Tom put in.

A floor man was immediately dispatched on the errand. Slade and Carvel found a table in the saloon and sat down, with coffee for Slade and a snort for old

148

Tom, to await the sheriff's arrival. Gypsy joined them. She smiled at her uncle and old Tom grinned. He glanced around, nodded approval.

'See you sorta fixed the place up after you took over,' he said. 'Not bad. How's business?'

'Nothing to complain about, Uncle Tom,' the girl replied.

'Good!' said old Tom. 'Good! Hope, though, you can find time to get out to the ranch now and then.'

'I will,' Gypsy promised.

Old Tom turned to Slade, 'Son,' he reminded, 'you said you'd explain why you didn't think those hellions were farmers.'

'I will, a little later, after the sheriff gets here,' Slade answered.

The sheriff arrived very shortly. He stared at Carvel unbelievingly.

'So you're here, eh?' he voiced the obvious.

'Well,' old Tom explained apologetically, 'Slade told me to get the hell in here and I figured I'd better.'

'And for once in your terrapin-brained life you used good judgment,' Orton declared. 'Otherwise he'd have very likely took you by the scruff of your neck and the seat of the pants and throwed you in.'

'I figured something like that and didn't argue with him,' old Tom admitted.

'All right, tell me what happened,' said the sheriff.

Old Tom told him, vividly and without reservation. 'And if it wasn't for him, I figured I'd have been a gone goslin',' he concluded, nodding at Slade.

'The chances are you would have been,' Orton agreed. 'I had some fellers pack that carcass to my office,' he said to Slade. 'Be a deputy there keepin' an eye on it. I ain't taking any chances after what happened to those first two.'

'I want to have a look at it,' Slade said. 'Come along, Mr. Carvel. I'll be back soon,' he promised Gypsy.

In the office, Slade examined the body of the slain outlaw with care. He was of

150

medium height and weight with a muddy complexion and eyes that in life had been squinty. Nothing outstanding about him so far as the Ranger could ascertain.

'Border scum,' was his verdict. 'The kind that will take over any kind of a chore, no matter how ornery, for hire. Come here a moment, Mr. Carvel. Bend close and take a look at this fellow's hands. Would you say those scars on them, not recent, but perfectly plain, were made by a farmer's shovel or pitchfork?'

Old Tom shook his head. 'Nope,' he admitted. 'Them are rope and brandin' iron burns.'

'You will concede then that he wasn't a farmer?' Slade persisted.

'Nope, he wasn't a farmer,' Carvel admitted, but, argumentative to the last, 'maybe the farmers hired the scut to do their shootin' for them.'

Slade let the full force of his cold eyes rest on the rancher's face.

'And would you say, sir, that those hill country farmers are the sort who would hire somebody to do their fighting for them?'

'No, blast it!' old Torn growled grudgingly. 'They may be mean and ornery, but I calc'late they do their own fightin'. But what the devil does it mean?'

'It means for one thing,' Slade replied quietly, 'that when honest men fall out, owlhoots move in. Somebody is deliberately trying to stir up trouble in this section, and you, and others like you, by your outmoded stubbornness and your refusal to admit progress, and your callous disregard for the rights of others, are furthering their ends. And I think we've had about enough of it. In the course of the — next few days, I'm going to pay you a visit at your *casa*, and you and I are going to take a little ride.'

'Okay,' Carvel sighed resignedly. 'As Gyp said, there's nothin' to be gained by arg'fyin' with you.'

Sheriff Orton chuckled. 'Darned if you ain't getting almost sensible in your old age,' he said. 'Wouldn't have believed it possible. Walt, one thing to be said for these sidewinders you keep downin', they sure enrich the county treasury, Look at the *dinero* this one was packin'! A heck of a sight more than he ever earned followin' a cow's tail. Nothing else in his pockets that amounts to anything, so far as I can see. I picked up his gun down there on the street, a good iron. Want it for a souvenir?'

'You keep it,' Slade replied. 'Well, I guess this is all we can do here.'

'And I'm headin' for The Widow Maker to let the boys see I'm all right,' said old Tom. 'See you tomorrow, son?'

'Yes,' Slade smiled, 'I'll meet you at Gypsy's place.'

'Fine! Come along, Brad, I feel the need of a snort and you always do.'

Gypsy's place had emptied out and only one dim light burned when Slade arrived, but she was waiting for him.

'Darling, you're wonderful!' she greeted. 'You said that before,' he pointed out.

'And I mean it just as much this time as I did then,' she replied. 'I wouldn't have dreamed that anyone could make Uncle Tom change his mind as you did.'

'It wasn't altogether me,' Slade said, 'Things just seemed to work out. I've learned that when one really needs help, something will usually reach down a hand to give it.'

'Yes,' she agreed softly. 'When one needs and *deserves* help. Wait till I lock the door. It's been a busy night, after all, and a very happy one.'

13

As he ate breakfast, around noon, Slade thought over the situation as it stood. Although his main problem appeared as far from solution as ever, he felt he had accomplished something. He was confident that he had swung old Tom Carvel into line, and very probably the other owners would follow his lead, he being the biggest and most influential of them. So at least he wouldn't have a range war on his hands to distract him and could concentrate on the paramount issue.

Who the devil was doing everything possible to delay the railroad construction, and why? The M.K. system appeared the logical culprit but, if so, he was very much of the opinion that somebody had gotten completely out of hand and was going it on his own. Why? Another question he wouldn't yet answer. Well it was up to him to find out; that was what he was here for.

'Why so serious, dear, and where have you been?' Gypsy asked. 'You were a million miles away and had forgotten me completely.'

'How could I with you sitting across the table from me, a vision of loveliness,' he denied. 'You are very charming in that dress that matches the color of your eyes. Almost as charming as with — '

'You talk too much!' she interrupted, silencing him with rosy fingertips. 'Be good, now, and eat your breakfast. Here comes Uncle Tom.'

Old Tom weaved across the floor looking somewhat worse for a busy night, but cheerful.

'Helped the boys close the darn place,' he explained. 'Lafe Moore, the owner, broke down and helped, too. The last I remember of *him*, he was asleep under a table with a table cloth for cover. He was a soldier for a long time and when he's had a few too many he figures he's campaignin' again and insists on sleepin' on the floor. Thinks a tablecloth — is a military cloak. Yep, it was quite a night, everything figured. Doubt if I can eat a bite. Waiter! A double order of hog hip and cackle berries!'

Gypsy ambled to the back room, where she had work to do. Slade sat with old Tom while he put away his double order of ham and eggs with appetite apparently unimpaired by his overnight potation.

'That helped,' he said, pushing back his empty plate. 'Now for a snort to bold it down and I'll be all set. What you aim to do, son?'

'I'm riding over to the railroad in a little while,' Slade answered.

'Okay,' nodded Carvel, downing the drink the waiter brought him. 'And I think I'll round up my boys and head for home — work to do. You'll be out to my place soon?'

'Within a day or two,' Slade promised.

'Good!' said Carvel, standing up. 'I'll say so long to Gyp and then trail my twine.'

He entered the back room, where he remained for some time. When he came out he looked even more cheerful. With a wave of his hand he was gone.

Gypsy rejoined Slade. 'He's happier than I've ever known him to be,' she said, apropos of old Tom. 'Yes, you did a wonderful thing, for both of us. What now, dear?'

'I'm heading for the railroad,' he replied. 'I'll be seeing you before long.'

'I hope so,' she said, 'and please be careful. You seem to be always getting into some kind of trouble.'

'I'll make out,' he answered cheerfully. 'Don't worry about me.'

'I'll try not to,' she promised. But the expression in her eyes as they followed him through the swinging doors told that she did worry.

When Slade reached the railroad, he found Jaggers Dunn in a cheerful mood.

'Everything's going smoothly,' he said. 'Nothing bad has happened and the work's going ahead.'

Slade nodded, but he experienced an uneasy premonition that it was the calm before the storm.

He was right.

'I'm going for a little ride,' he announced. 'See you to night or tomorrow.'

Dunn glanced at him curiously but asked no questions. Slade did take a ride, a twelve-mile ride southwest to Hamon, the farmers' town. He rode at a fast pace and .got there in the late afternoon.

Hamon had no saloons, which was perhaps the reason some of the younger farmers occasionally made the trip to Oresta. However, Slade had no difficulty locating a big and airy restaurant that was spotlessly clean. He dropped the split reins to the ground beside a hitchrack, entered, and ordered coffee and a sandwich. Several other diners glanced at him questioningly, evidently taking in his rangeland garb, but did not address him. He spoke to the waiter who served him, a friendly and loquacious individual, gradually leading the conversation to the subject he was interested in.

'Who is the head man of the farmers, do you know?' Slade finally asked.

'Why, Bije Manning usually tells them what to do. He runs the general store, just a hop and a skip down the street. A nice feller, Bije.'

Slade thanked the waiter, paid his check, and strolled out, while eyes followed his progress. When he entered the general store there was nobody present save a pleasant-faced, elderly man behind the counter. He had a humorous mouth and shrewd blue eyes that regarded the Ranger inquiringly.

'Mr. Manning?' Slade asked as he approached the counter. 'That's right,' said the other. 'Reckon you have the advantage of me.'

Slade supplied his name and they shook hands. 'What can I do for you, son?' Manning asked.

'A favor,' Slade replied smiling.

Manning looked puzzled, but his reply was ready. 'Certain, anything I can do. What is it?'

'I would like to bring a friend to have a little talk with you,' *El Halcón* explained. 'A Mr. Thomas Carvel.'

Bije Manning's eyes widened a trifle. 'Carvel,' he repeated. 'He's the big feller of the cattlemen hereabouts, ain't he? Don't seem to have much use for us fellers.'

'I think you will find,' Slade answered, his smile broadening, 'that Mr. Carvel has undergone a change of heart. Which I feel safe in assuming goes for the other cowmen, too. He would like to make amends and forget past differences.'

Bije Manning looked a bit bewildered. 'Why — why this is sorta surprising and unexpected,' he said. 'But if Carvel feels that way about it, I don't see any reason why we can't get along.'

'Exactly,' Slade said. 'No reason why you can't be good neighbors, which will certainly work to the advantage of both.'

For a moment the storekeeper was silent, regarding Slade curiously.

'Son,' he said at length, 'you're a strange young feller. Somehow when you say a thing you make a man believe it's so.'

'Thank you, Mr. Manning,' the

Ranger replied, suddenly flashing the white smile of *El Halcón*. 'And I assure you that in this case what I tell you is so.'

'I sure don't doubt it,' Manning said, and chuckled. He glanced around, produced a bottle from under the counter.

'The deacons don't approve of likkersellin' in town,' he said, 'but most of us like a little nip now and then.' With which he took two glasses from a shelf and filled them to the brim.

Slade chatted for some little time with the storekeeper before heading back east, learning a good deal about the farmers and their plans.

'Bring Mr. Carvel around whenever you're of a mind to,' Manning said in parting. 'And,' he added, 'I've got a prime notion you were responsible for his change of heart. I figure you kinda enlightened him, maybe sorta as Pharaoh was enlightened.'

'Not exactly,' Slade smiled in reply. 'Pharaoh experienced many tribulations before *he* saw the light. Mr. Carvel only suffered a skinned head.'

With which he was gone, leaving Bije Manning even more bewildered than before.

'Well, horse,' he said to Shadow as he rode through the blue and gold of the twilight, 'I've a notion we did a pretty good chore today. I believe we paved the way for a peaceful settlement of the controversy between the cowmen and the farmers. Which ought to help, and maybe it will help us with the other chore, the one that brought us to this section. I hope so, for I'm becoming a mite weary of chasing my tail around in circles and getting exactly nowhere.'

He rode on, singing softly in his deep, rich voice and, for a change, feeling remarkably carefree.

But as he sighted the lights of Oresta and the more scattered and dimmed lights of the railroad yards, he experienced an unexplainable feeling of anxiety, a feeling he had experienced before when something was not just right. It strengthened as he continued on his way.

So strong did it become that he

abruptly turned north from the Oresta trail, toward the yards.

'Maybe I'm just loco, horse, but I'm playing a hunch,' he said. 'Things have been going smoothly for the past few days and it's just possible that folks have been lulled into a false security. Anyhow, old Jaggers may still be up and, if so, we'll drop in on him for a few minutes before heading to town.'

The course he followed took him to the east end of the yards where the nearly completed roundhouse and machine-shop were located. He reached the little stable where Shadow had been domiciled and pulled to a halt. Dismounting, he dropped the split reins to the ground.

'Stay put, I'm going to snoop around a little,' he told the horse, and proceeded to do so, cautiously, hoping some trigger nervous yard policeman wouldn't take a shot at him, a contingency he thought remote. They were quite probably holed up in their shanty, not being much given to prowling around in the dark. He sighted the private car, which was dark, as were the nearby camp cars where the workers slept. Directly ahead loomed the gaunt building that housed the machine shop.

He rounded a corner of the structure and saw, a score of paces ahead, a flickering light which almost instantly strengthened to a leaping glow that revealed the figures of three men straightening up from a crouch.

And *El Halcón* understood! His voice rang out, 'Elevatet. You're covered!'

The three whirled toward the sound of his voice with startled exclamations. A gun blazed and the bullet fanned the Ranger's face. He drew and shot with both hands.

A gasping cry echoed the reports and a man fell forward toward the fire. The others darted into the darkness, shooting as they ran. Slade bounded forward, tripped over something on the ground, reeled off balance and almost fell. As he recovered he heard the thud of fast hoofs fading into the distance.

Heaped against the building was a

huge heap of oil-soaked cotton waste blazing fiercely, the flames licking up the tinder dry wooden wall of the machine shop which was already beginning to smolder.

Slade's great voice rolled in thunder through the night. 'Turn out! Turn out! Fire! Fire!' He accompanied his shouts with a salvo of shots in the general direction of the fleeing horsemen.

14

Voices sounded from the aroused camp cars. Men came tumbling out in all stages of undress. Though dazed with sleep, those experienced workers knew exactly what to do. Within minutes a bucket brigade was formed, A hose was hooked to the mud valve of a locomotive and a stream of water played on the flames which were rapidly eating their way to the roof of the building. Jaggers Dunn came roaring into the tumult to direct operations.

For minutes it was touch and go, but gradually the fire fighters gained the ascendency. The flames sank, flickered, then turned to glowing patches and sparks which were finally extinguished. Flares and torches were lighted and the damage inspected and found to be not serious.

The arsonist Slade shot had fallen into the fire and his body was burned beyond human semblance. Jaggers Dunn solemnly shook hands with Slade, while the smoke-and-ash-blackened workers raised a cheer.

'Right on the job, as usual, eh?' chortled the G.M. 'I knew darn well you were when your guns cut loose. Well, if it wasn't for you, right now we'd be in big trouble. That blasted fire would have very likely spread to all the bulidings. How in blazes did you catch on?'

'Played a hunch,' Slade replied. 'Had a feeling I'd better look around a bit before continuing to town. Hunch paid off.' 'It sure did,' growled Dunn. 'But I got another name for it. Seems you think of everything, in advance. I don't see how the devil you do it.'

'It was just that I didn't feel right about things being so peaceful of late,' Slade explained. 'Seemed to me it was about time they made another try.'

'And the rest of us were too blasted smug and satisfied with the way thinks were going,' said Dunn. 'Come on and have some coffee.'

'I'll look after my horse first,' Slade replied. 'Time for him to put on the nosebag.'

'I'll walk with you,' Dunn offered.

The stablekeeper was up and around, so Shadow was quickly taken care of.

'Coffee and snack comin' up, Boss man,' announced the imperturbable Sam as they entered the coach.

'Nothing ever excites him,' snorted Jaggers. 'Build a fire under him and he'd just get up and walk away without saying a word.'

'Takes more'n a little smoke to scare me,' said Sam as he headed for the kitchen.

They were just sitting down at the table when Sheriff Orton loomed in the door.

'Well let's hear about it,' he said, joining them at the table.

Slade told him, Jaggers adding a few pungent remarks of his own.

'So! Barbecued bandit for a change, eh?' remarked the sheriff. 'Well, it sorta busts up the monotony.'

'And if it hadn't been for Slade, it would have just about busted up a railroad yard,' growled Dunn. 'Next would have been the roundhouse and half a dozen engines, and the turn table and the camp cars. We'd have been out of business for quite a while.'

'Now what?' he asked, after Sam's offering was consumed. 'I'm riding to town,' Slade said. 'Promised somebody I'd try and be back tonight.'

'Me, too,' agreed the sheriff. 'I'll send somebody with a roasting pan to gather up the remains, Mr. Dunn.'

'Not much left of the hellion, but okay,' nodded the G.M. 'Be seeing you, Walt, and much obliged again for everything.' Before leaving, Slade instituted a search for the dead arsonist's horse. It was not found; had evidently followed the others when the fellow's two companions fled.

Reaching town and stabling his horse, Slade repaired to Gypsy Carvel's place. She greeted him resignedly.

'I know very well you were mixed up in it somehow,' she said. 'We heard there was a shooting and a fire over at the railroad yard. What happened?'

Chuckling at her perspicacity, Slade recounted the incident.

She shook her curly head.

'Just let you out of my sight and you are in trouble!' she declared. 'What next?'

'Tomorrow I hope for peace and quiet,' he replied. 'I'm just riding out to your uncle's place. Expect I'll stay there tomorrow night.'

'I see,' she said. A smile twitched her red lips and she regarded him with laughing eyes.

'I guarantee something happens to you,' she said. Slade looked puzzled, but she said no more.

He did ride the next day. The trail ran over excellent rangeland, with fat beefs cropping the luxuriant grass growth. Finally he sighted Tom Carvel's *casa*, a big white house surrounded by tightly constructed outbuildings, all in good repair. A setting commensurate to the owner's wealth and standing. Old Tom came out onto the veranda as Slade approached

171

and after greeting him warmly, bellowed for a wrangler who came running and was introduced to Shadow.

'A small helping of oats and water,' Slade directed. 'Don't remove the rig, just flip the bit and loosen the cinches; I'll be wanting him shortly.'

Old Tom shot him a glance but did not comment. 'Come on in,' he invited. 'Coffee and snack will be ready pronto.' Following him into the big living room, Slade received an impression of comfort that verged on luxury. Among other furnishings, a massive grand piano caught his eye. Carvel noted the direction of his gaze and remarked, 'My wife played real well. Gyp doesn't do so bad, either. Take a load off your feet and make yourself comfortable.'

'You have a fine piece of property, sir,' Slade commented.

'Yes, it's a good holding,' Carvel admitted. He sighed. 'I'd hoped to have a kid to leave it to, but somehow one never came to us,' he said. 'Yes, it's a good holding, but it gets sorta lonesome at times, since

Gyp walked out on me, and no kid to sorta make things livelier and to inherit it after I'm gone.'

His pale eyes hard on the old rancher's face, Slade spoke, his voice deep and musical.

'Ever occur to you, Mr. Carvel,' he remarked casually, 'that other men might cherish a like ambition and strive to get some of the good this great land of ours has to offer, so that they can pass it on to *their* sons and daughters? And are willing to work and strive and endure hardship to that end? And that a helping hand from the right direction, instead of spite and opposition, might mean a great deal to them?'

Old Tom suddenly flushed. 'I get what you mean, I reckon,' he replied. 'Guess you're thinking of the farmers.'

Slade noticed the use of the word 'farmers' instead of 'nesters' and smiled slightly.

'I am,' he said, and there was a subtle reproof in his deep tones.

Old Tom tugged his mustache and

observed, with apparent irrelevance, 'I been talking with some of the boys — the other owners — and they sorta see things the way you put it the other night. Sorta changing their notions about the farmers, after I dropped a hint or two.'

Slade bit back a smile with difficulty. He had a pretty good notion concerning the 'hints' dropped by the influential Carvel, the acknowledged leader of the cattlemen.

Old Tom again seemed to change the subject. 'The other night you said something about you and me taking a ride to-gether,' he remarked. 'Over the spread?'

'No,' Slade replied, this time letting the smile really appear, the devils of laughter in his eyes edging to the front. 'No, to Hamon.'

Carvel looked startled. 'To Hamon!' he repeated. 'Sure they won't take a shotgun to us over there?'

'I think we can risk it,' Slade returned composedly.

Old Tom was silent for a while, then

abruptly he said, 'I reckon the old are set in their ways, and sorta selfish, at times. Maybe just thoughtless and living inside themselves too much.'

'But they don't need to remain selfish and self-centered,' Slade replied gently.

'Guess you're right, per usual,' Carvel said. 'Yes, guess you're right.'

They finished their coffee and snack. Carvel glanced suggestively at Slade.

'Ready to hightail?' he asked. 'Let's go,' the Ranger answered.

They rode at a good pace and did not draw rein until they reached Hamon. Leaving their horses at a nearby rack, they entered the general store. Bije Manning was behind the counter and voiced a greeting. Slade performed the introductions.

Old Tom was impulsive and he said, without preamble,

'Manning, I came here to eat a little crow. Guess us fellers over on the range haven't acted just right to you fellers. Slade sorta opened our eyes for us. So I just wanted to know if we can't forget our past differences, stop squabblin' and be good neighbors to each other.'

'Brother Carvel,' Manning replied in the words of a great general, 'let us have peace.'

They shook hands again, solemnly.

Manning was from Virginia and old Tom's grandfather had been born and brought up there, so soon the two old-sters were reminiscing and discussing people and places. Slade listened for a while and then announced, 'I'm going for a walk. Be seeing you a little later.' The pair nodded absently and went on talking.

Slade wandered around the town for a while, finding it clean and orderly and with a prosperous air. The farmers were true home builders. After a while he entered the big restaurant for some coffee. Evidently Manning had been spreading talk around, for several patrons greeted him with friendly nods and the loquacious waiter acknowledged him as an old acquaintance. Finishing his coffee, he returned to the general store.

'Guess we'd better be moving,' he told Carvel. 'Be dark before we reach home as it is.'

'Yes, reckon we'd better,' agreed old Tom. 'Be seeing you, Bije, and don't forget.'

'I won't,' Manning promised. 'It will be a pleasure, brother. And thank you, Brother Slade, for everything.'

'He's got a lot of thanks coming from all of us,' Carvel declared. Manning nodded solemn agreement.

'Bije is quite a feller,' old Tom remarked as they headed for the ranch house. 'I asked him to come over to dinner one night this week and bring along some friends if he was of a mind to. He said he would.'

'That was nice of you, and a very good idea,' Slade said.

As they rode into the yard, they heard somebody playing the piano, quite well, Slade thought.

'Now who the devil can that be?' wondered old Tom. 'None of the boys can tickle a music box, that's sure for certain.'

Slade smiled, for he had a very good notion as to who it was.

The wrangler came hurrying to care for the horses and, after removing his saddle pouches, Slade and the rancher entered the casa. Gypsy, as Slade expected, turned from the piano to greet them. Old Tom's eyes brightened.

'Gyp!' he exclaimed. 'Say! It's fine to see you.'

Gypsy laughed and turned to Slade. 'You told me you intended to spend the night here so I followed you,' she said. 'You can't get away from me as easily as all that. At least for a while,' she added, her eyes suddenly wistful.

'Maybe we can arg'fy him into coiling his twine here,' old Tom insinuated.

'Uncle Tom, you can't cage an eagle' she replied. 'Or a hawk, either, for that matter. But go wash up, you two, your dinner will be ready by the time you are. Show him the bathroom, Uncle Tom. I'll give Pete a hand in the kitchen.'

'Fetch along your pouches and we'll chuck 'em in your room,' said Carvel.

'We're sorta old-fashioned in some ways but in others we ain't,' he added as they climbed the stairs.

'Got a real bathroom. Tank on top of the house, hydraulic ram fills it from a spring. Beats a wash pan in back.'

He opened a door near the head of the stairs and the hall lights revealed a comfortably furnished room in which Slade deposited his saddle pouches.

'I sleep in the back of the house, in case you want some thing during the night,' old Tom announced. 'Gyp has the room across the hall from you.'

After enjoying an excellent dinner, they returned to the living room. Gypsy glanced toward the piano.

'Walt,' she said, 'Miguel, my cook, told me you play and that you have a wonderful voice. Won't you sing for us, please?'

'Guess I can stand it if you can,' Slade replied. He adjusted the stool to his liking, sat down, and ran his fingers over the keys with a master's touch. For a few moments his slender bands weaved soft harmonies from the instrument, which was a really good one. Then he threw back his black head and sang.

The wild hawk to the wind-swept sky,
The wolf to his earthbound thrall,
And the heart of a man to the open road
When he harks to the red gods' call!

And as the great golden voice pealed and thundered through the room, Gypsy sat with wide eyes, her red lips parted, her hands trembling a little.

The music ceased in a whisper of exquisite melody. Slade turned and smiled at her. But her answering smile was tremulous.

'Just a minute,' said old Tom. 'The boys got to have a share in this.'

He opened the door and let out a bellow. Soon the hands came trooping from the bunkhouse, looking expectant.

So Slade sang several numbers for them. Songs of the hills and the plains, of the drowsing herd and the lonely campfire, of the horse and the dog and the men who love both.

'The singingest man in the whole Southwest, with the fastest gunhand!' murmured Bill Weston. 'Gents, them are true words.'

'And a man to ride the river with,' said big Hunch.

'Yep, the good old Cimarron in flood,' added another hand amid sober nods of agreement.

Later, after the bunkhouse was dark and old Tom had ambled off to bed, when everything was peaceful and quiet,

Gypsy sat, chin in pink palm and regarded Slade for several minutes.

'And the heart of a man to the open road,' she quoted softly. 'Yes, that is it, the only thing that can hold your heart for long, the heart of a wanderer.'

'Not exactly,' he replied. 'Come here.'

She did so and perched on his knee. From a cunningly concealed secret pocket in his broad leather belt he took something that caught the light, a gleaming silver star set on a silver circle, the feared and honored badge of the Texas Rangers.

'Not exactly an aimless wanderer, you see,' he said.

For a long moment she gazed at the symbol of law and order and justice for all.

'Yes, I see,' she said. 'You do have a definite mission, and perhaps the day may come when you will really settle down.'

'Yes,' he said.

Again she was silent, then abruptly her bright smile flashed. 'It's late,' she said. 'Blow out the light and let's see if we can climb the stairs in the dark without falling on our heads. And without awakening Uncle Tom,' she added, with a giggle.

15

The next day, after seeing Gypsy safe in her establishment, Slade rode to the railroad yards and found Jaggers Dunn in a roaring bad temper.

'Gosh-blast it! You were right, as usual,' he bawled, waving a sheet of yellow paper under Slade's nose. 'Look at this!' Slade took the sheet and read the laconic message from one of Dunn's trusted subordinates, 'M.K. building north.' 'And I've got to leave for Chicago in the morning to at tend a directors' meeting I can't afford to miss!' raved the G.M. 'Well, I guess you'll have to take over while I'm gone — I'll be gone a week at least. You know, McNelty won't mind.'

'No, Captain Jim won't mind, and it looks like I'd be sticking around the railroad most of the time anyhow,' Slade replied. 'But maybe Mr. Becker won't like it. He's the engineer in charge, you know.'

'I don't give a blankety-blank-blank what anybody likes or don't like!' stormed Jaggers. 'You are the only person I can trust to do the right thing, conditions being what they are. If Becker has any objections, he can take the first train east. Here's your authority — you've had it before.'

He grabbed a pen and paper and began scratching away in handwriting like a barbed wire railing, appending his signature.

'There you are,' he repeated, passing the paper to Slade.

The Ranger folded it and carefully stowed it away.

'I won't use it unless I feel the need to,' he said. 'So don't mention it to Becker or anybody else.'

'Anything you say,' growled Jaggers. 'Now sit down with me and I'll give you a line — up on certain details, although the chances are you're familiar with them already. You always seem to know everything.'

They talked for more than an hour, Slade asking numerous questions that Jaggers answered. Finally he said, 'Well, I guess that covers everything. And you expect to be back in a week or so?'

'I hope so,' Jaggers corrected. 'There's a big deal in the making that may take more time to consummate — tell you all about that when I get back — and it could hold me longer.' 'Okay,' Slade said, 'if we reach Hamon before you return, I'll start the survey lines west to Randal. May do so before no reason for secrecy any longer. I know the country over there and only minor difficulties should be encountered, I hope.'

'Whatever you think best,' agreed Jaggers. 'You'll be in charge. I only wish you'd drop the Rangers and come in with me like I want you to.'

He spoke hopefully, but even as he voiced the words, he saw Slade's eyes look up and off toward the far horizon and beyond. He sighed and let the subject drop.

'I'm going out and walk around a bit,'

Slade said. 'Want to look things over a little.'

'Okay,' nodded Jaggers, turning to his desk. 'I got quite a bit of work to do. Be seeing you.'

Sauntering about, studying certain details of the yard construction, Slade paused before the scorched wall of the machine shop, which was undergoing repairs. He understood that Sheriff Orton had already buried the roasted body of the arsonist. Despite the hellion's orneriness, he hoped the bullet had killed him and that he had not been forced to endure the torture of the flames. Not a very nice way to die.

From the corner of his eye, Slade saw a man approaching. He waited till a hand touched his shoulder and turned to face Howard Becker, the field engineer in charge of the project. Becker smiled his thin — lipped gray smile.

'How are you, Mr. Slade?' he said. 'I heard about it. Was in town when it happened. I gather that had it not been for you, the whole yard would have very likely gone up in smoke.'

'Oh, not that bad I'd say,' Slade deprecated the part he played in the incident. 'The boys are very efficient and would probably have gotten it under control.'

'Not if it had gotten a head start, which it would have done had you not interrupted the scheme,' Becker disagreed. 'We have to congratulate ourselves that you happened to be around at so timely a moment. As it is, no real damage was done. Thank you, Mr. Slade.'

He smiled again, the wintry smile that never seemed to reach his keen, dark blue eyes that in certain lights appeared to be black.

'I won't forget what you did,' he added. 'Be seeing you work to do.' He moved on, his step lithe, assured, his bearing that of the able and adroit man he undoubtedly was. Slade watched him go, then turned his attention elsewhere.

For a couple of hours, he wandered about the yard inspecting the various activities and was satisfied with all he saw. Becker was an engineer, all right, and a good one. And his calm, aloof personality achieved respect from even the turbulent workers who were not noted for sweetness and light and usually packed a whole basketful of chips on their brawny shoulders.

They were doing very well, but Slade thought that given the proper incentive they could do even better. Respect for a boss made for efficiency, but not the drive and the fierce loyalty they would give to one they really admired and liked. Despite his undoubted ability, Howard Becker would never be a man to lead a lost cause against impossible odds — and win.

Very well satisfied with everything he saw, Slade returned to the private car. In the next day or two he would ride to the railhead which was pushing west at a good pace.

He found Jaggers Dunn tying up loose ends and making preparations for his trip to Chicago.

'Will be pulling out first thing tomorrow morning,' he said. 'Well, I'm leaving with a free mind. All my worries dumped on your shoulders.'

'Hope I won't disappoint you,' Slade smiled. 'Big chance!' Dunn snorted. 'Now what?'

Slade glanced at the westering sun. 'I'm riding to town,' he announced 'Will be back here in the morning sometime. Have a good trip. So long, Sam,' he added to the porter. 'Be seeing you.'

After arriving in town and stabling his horse, Slade made his way to The Widow Maker where, as he expected, he found Sheriff Orton eating his dinner. Sitting down with coffee, he regaled the peace officer with an account of the previous day's happenings. Orton shook his head resignedly. 'So you got the hellions together, eh?' he remarked. 'I don't know how you do it! I don't know how you do it!'

However, the sheriff did know. Through the naked power of his stalwart manhood, his outstanding personality, and his firm belief in the right.

When Slade arrived at Gypsy's place,

he got something of a surprise. At the bar, a number of young farmers were conversing amiably with a bunch of cowhands. Evidently the word had gotten around fast.

He was not really much surprised. He knew that the punchers took little interest in their employers' feud with the farmers and the railroad. They followed the boss's lead as a matter of course, but with scant personal enthusiasm. They were glad to have peace and the opportunity to relax and enjoy themselves.

A waving of hands from both groups greeted his entrance and by the time he sat down at a table, two filled glasses were before him, one from each bunch. He raised one in acknowledgment and smiled.

'So! Well on the way to getting drunk already, eh?' Gypsy said as she plumped into a chair beside him. 'I think I will, too.'

'Not a bad idea,' Slade agreed. 'Might get novel results' 'Not satisfied with me as I am?'

'What do you think?' he countered.

'Well,' she replied, dimpling and smiling, 'I'm certainly not complaining.'

When Slade rode to the railroad the next day, a couple of hours before noon, the spur which had been occupied by the private car was empty; Jaggers Dunn was on his way to Chicago. Hooking a long leg comfortably over the saddle horn, he rolled a cigarette and pondered the situation. Everything about the yards appeared to be going smoothly, so after a bit he arrived at a decision. Pinching out the butt he rode west along the course of the newly laid tracks, toward the railhead, which was now only some seven or eight miles from Hamon.

When he reached the railhead, another surprise was in store for him. The track layers were busy at their chores, but sitting their horses nearby or riding around on the prairie were half a dozen cowhands and as many young farmers. They waved a greeting. Slade approached the track gang foreman. 'Were here when we started work,' that worthy chuckled, apropos of the punchers and the farmers. 'They say they're standin' guard over the line, day and night, from now on, to make sure nobody tries any shenanigans.'

Slade smiled, for in it he saw the hands of Bije Manning and old Tom Carvel. He rode over and spoke to the watchers, thanking them for their thoughtfulness. Then, in a complacent frame of mind, he rode on west, following the line of survey stakes that marched sedately across the rangeland slanting slightly to the south, as they should.

His complacency was short-lived. Very soon it was a thing of the past. Some four miles to the west he reached a point where the prairie ahead abruptly changed. Directly ahead was a stretch upon which no tree grew. There was a luxurious stand of grass, but grass radically different from that clothing the rest of the prairie. It was of a peculiar jaundiced green somewhat similar to the grass of the salt marshes along the Gulf of Mexico coast. Upon it no cattle fed, although Slade saw bunches grazing nearby.

The stretch was a mile or a little more wide, by some three miles in length, north and south. And across its middle the stakes marking the survey line marched steadily on.

Slade's lips pursed in a low — whistle. He spoke to Shadow and the big black moved on. But he didn't like it. He snorted protest and raised and lowered his hoofs gingerly.

'Don't worry,' Slade told him. 'It will hold *you*.'

However, after a few score paces of listening intently to the sound of the horse's footfalls, he turned back, drew rein and again sat gazing across the verdant expanse. With an exclamation, he turned Shadow's nose and rode north at a fast pace. He passed the strange appearing stretch but continued in line with it as the hills drew nearer.

As he approached their base, a murmuring sound came to his ears, a sound that gradually loudened and which he identified as the moan and mutter of falling water. A little later he saw it was caused by a small stream that tumbled down from the hills.

But the stream did not continue across the rangeland. Instead, it boiled into an opening in the rocks and vanished from sight. Slade pulled Shadow to a halt.

'Just as I expected, horse,' he said. 'And all of a sudden everything is perfectly clear. Okay, feller, let's go.'

Loosening the reins, he rode swiftly east until he reached the railroad yards. There he had no difficulty locating Howard Becker, the engineer, sitting his horse and watching a track laying operation. Slade drew rein beside him.

'Mr. Becker,' he said quietly, 'please come with me; I have something to show you.'

The engineer stared at him. 'I'm very busy right now, Mr. Slade,' he objected.

'Please come with me,' the Ranger repeated. Evidently the icy glitter in his eyes convinced Becker it was best to obey.

'All right,' he said.

In silence, they rode steadily westward until Slade drew rein on the edge of the yellow-tinged grass. He pointed to the line of stakes.

'Mr. Becker,' he said, 'the road will not cross here. It will veer to the south and bypass that stretch by way of a sweeping curve that will gradually merge with the survey line *beyond* that stretch.'

Becker stared at him and his gray face flushed slightly. 'Mr. Slade,' he said angrily, 'who are you to tell me what to do? I am in charge here.'

By way of answer, Slade handed him a folded sheet of paper. The engineer unfolded it and read, over the indubitable signature of General Manager James G. Dunn. 'To all officials and other employees of the C. & P. Railroad System:

'Orders given by the bearer, Walter J. Slade, will be obeyed without question, to the letter, and at once.'

16

Becker raised his eyes to Slade, and they seemed to have darkened.

'Does this mean I am discharged?' he asked thickly. 'No, Mr. Becker,' Slade replied. 'It means just what it says, that I am absolutely in charge here, subject only to the check of Mr. Dunn, when he is present. Mr. Becker, every one makes mistakes, and you made one here. Evidently you are not familiar with conditions that exist here. I am. Under that marsh grass and a not very thick rind of eroded earth is a bottomless slough, a quagmire. The surface earth will bear no great weight. You may notice that nowhere does a tree grow on that expanse. The quag would not — permit it. You couldn't run even a material train across that thing with out it being engulfed.'

'I — I think you are mistaken,' Becker said. 'I ran the line across there and I am convinced it is run as it should be. I think you are wrong.'

'I am not wrong,' Slade stated flatly. 'And the responsibility is mine. Get your survey gang together and run the survey as I tell you. With the line never less than two hundred yards from the edge of the quag. I really don't think so, but there is always the possibility of it eating its way farther under the prairie, during flood time. So we will take no chances. Run the line exactly as I tell you.'

'Very well,' Becker agreed. 'It would appear I have no choice in the matter.' He regarded Slade curiously for a moment.

'You have worked with Mr. Dunn before?' he asked. 'I have,' Slade replied.

'His trouble shooter, I presume?'

'You may call it that,' Slade conceded, for it was near enough the truth.

'Very well,' Becker repeated. 'I'll do as you say, at once.'

He turned his horse and rode east without a backward glance. Slade rolled a cigarette and watched his progress until he had dwindled out of sight.

'Shadow,' he remarked reflectively, 'I wonder if the hellion caught on? I wonder if he realizes that I *know* running of the survey line across that quag was not an accident due to ignorance but a deliberate attempt at sabotage. One that would, had it succeeded, put the quietus on the endeavor on the part of the C. & P. to reach Randal ahead of the M.K.? I don't think he caught on, but I'm not sure. If I was really working for Dunn, I'd just fire him and kick him off the right of — way. But I'm first and foremost a Texas Ranger, with a chore of Ranger work to do. That hellion is responsible for crimes against Texas law and must be brought to justice, one way or another. So we'll have to let him stick around where we can keep an eye on him, even against the chance of his making more trouble for the road.

'Yes, it was a deliberate attempt at slowing up the road construction. Any engineer of ability, such as Becker undoubtedly is, would recognize conditions here, or would at least have been highly suspicious of them. He would never have run a survey line across this thing without first taking experimental borings to see what was under that poisonous looking grass, and would have discovered the quag formed by that underground stream which somehow gets dammed for a while before rising enough to find an outlet by which it continues its course south. Well, at least now we know whom to look for, which is something. He's the M.K.'s man planted here, all right, and has gotten completely out of hand; he would have shaken them down for plenty had he succeeded in doing what he set out to do. They should have thought of that, but some folks seem never to learn.'

Although the afternoon was well along, Becker was as good as his word and less than two hours later reappeared with his survey bunch, via mule cart.

The transit man, rod man, chain men and stake men reagarded Slade curiously when — he designated the point where the change of direction should occur, but offered no comment. They got busy with efficiency and dispatch.

Satisfied that everything was under control, for the time being at least, Slade rode back to the yards. There he talked with several of the foremen, showing them Dunn's order. They were cordial and seemed pleased at the change of authority. Slade gathered from chance remarks that while Becker was respected, he was not liked.

After watching the foremen spreading the word among the workers, he stabled his horse and dropped in at the cook car for a cup of coffee. He chatted with the colored cook till the work day ended and the men came trooping in. He walked out, stood on the top step, and called them to attention. When all, or nearly all were assembled, he smiled down at the sea of expectant faces and got grins in return.

'Fellows,' he called, 'I have one or two things to say to you. In the first place, we are in a race. We're not going to stop at Hamon but will drive on west to Randal in New Mexico. The M.K. bunch is trying to get there first. Are we going to let them do it?'

'Like hell we are!' came an answering roar.

'Fine!' Slade applauded. 'I know I can depend on you. There'll be a lot of overtime from now on, but there'll be double pay for every hour of it. Not bad, eh?'

A cheer arose, and a forest of hands.

'Fellers, we ain't gonna let Mr. Slade down!' boomed a big Irish track foreman. 'He's a b'ye the Quid Sod could be proud of!'

Slade flashed his white smile, waved his hand and they dispersed, chattering animatedly.

'Boss man, you done got 'em' the cook chuckled behind him. 'They'll foller you to hell and twist the Devil's tail, if you ask 'em to!'

* * *

El Halcón rode to town through the glow of the twilight, pretty well satisfied with the day's work. He knew very well that his chore was far from finished; he didn't doubt but that shrewd and resourceful Becker still had a card or two up his sleeve. He knew, too, that grave personal danger for himself was involved. Becker had evidently brought a salty and ruthless bunch with him, men who would stop at nothing and who would do anything for pay. Well, he had encountered such conditions before and things had always worked out, so why bother! He rode on, whistling gaily and tweaking Shadow's ears to the accompaniment of equine profanity.

'Wonderful!' Gypsy exclaimed when he arrived at her place. 'Another night without gallivanting off somewhere?'

'Looks sorta that way,' Slade agreed.

'Sheriff Orton will be in shortly,' she said. 'Wants to see you, I think.'

The sheriff showed up a little later. Slade acquainted him with the latest developments. Orton expressed decided surprise.

'I don't like the gray-faced hellion — he's too darn uppity,' he said apropos of Howard Becker, 'but I'd never have figured him to be mixed up in some skullduggery. I've been sorta looking sideways at Jackson Dane, who's a good deal of a puzzler.'

'You can write him off, as I did some time ago,' Slade replied. 'He is just a shrewd article who took a gamble when he bought that land without knowing for sure the railroad would come through this way. As it is, he stands to cash in.'

'How's that?' Orton asked.

'In that section of the hills he bought from the state is, I believe, a very valuable copper deposit,' Slade explained. 'Texas doesn't produce much copper, you know, and there is a good local market. However, the former long wagon haul to the railroad would have been so expensive it is doubtful if mining the ore would have paid. But with the railroad only a few miles distant, Dane can either mine his ore or sell his holding at a handsome profit. Either way, I wouldn't be surprised if he runs cows onto his rangeland and sticks around. I think he likes it here.'

'I see,' nodded the sheriff. 'Well, good luck to him. And you don't think Becker has caught on to what you are and why you're here?'

'I don't believe he has, and I certainly hope he hasn't,' Slade answered. 'Right now I feel that he is very likely a mite puzzled. I'm sure he had me tagged as *El Halcón* planning to horn in on his scheme, perhaps by way of a little polite blackmail or something of the sort. At present I'd say he's not sure what to think. Not that he is finished, not by a long shot. He's smart as a treeful of owls and resourceful. We'll hear from him again, and unpleasantly, I predict. And the way the situation stands at present, I haven't a thing on him. He can claim running the survey line across the quag was just an honest mistake on his part, and nobody could prove otherwise. Well, we'll see.

'Strange, isn't it, that a man one would think has everything necessary to make a success of an honest life should take the wrong fork in the trail. The lure of easy money, I suppose. Jim Dunn is a hard one to fool, but Becker put it over on him. I'll admit that I never really regarded him as a possible suspect until this afternoon. He is the self-effacing sort, to whom you are not likely — to give a second glance. He stays back in the shadows, pulling the wires, a gray shadow amid the shadows, barely discernible as an entity. The hardest type for a law enforcement officer to run down. As I said, I haven't a thing on him that would stand up in court.'

'You'll get it,' the sheriff declared confidently. 'No doubt in my mind as to that. Well, here comes Gyp with our dinner. About time.'

Several uneventful days followed as the railroad went forward. The changed survey line was completed to Slade's satisfaction. There was plenty of overtime, pushing the steel to Hamon at the greatest possible speed. The workers knew they had a race on their hands and were determined to win it, and they were fiercely loyal to the new Big Boss.

'The Old Man's all right,' they were wont to say, employing the term they used to signify a boss they not only respected but liked, a term they had never applied to Howard Becker. 'Yep, he's okay. Always nice, always ready to listen to your beef about something, always ready to straighten things out for you. Always ready to lend a hand where it's needed. And is he a man! The other day a couple of the boys were having trouble getting a rail in line that was stuck. Mr. Slade just took hold of one end and by himself dropped it in place neat as a whistle. Sure wouldn't want to tangle with him. Betcha he could give a grizzly bear the underhold and come out on top! Yep, and he's the Big Boss, all right, but just the same he's one of the boys.'

Howard Becker was courteous and cooperative, never mentioning their initial difference. He did his work as it should be done, with efficiency and dispatch and did not question any of Slade's orders.

But Slade knew that all the while Becker was studying him, and he would have given much to be able to read what went on back of that gray, mask — like face. Becker was absolutely expression-less save for his eyes which he couldn't quite control. Now and then *El Halcón* surprised a hard glitter in their dark depths as they rested on him, and he became convinced that Becker was just biding his time, that he had something up his sleeve that he very likely regarded as an ace.

It did not take him long to discover that Becker, who never discarded his coat no matter how warm the day, wore a heavy gun in a shoulder holster under his left armpit, and the Ranger felt pretty sure that the engineer was a master at that difficult but very fast draw.

It was a deadly game they were play-ing, *El Halcón* well knew, and a little slip on his part might well prove fatal. How-ever, he had no intention of making a slip that would give the other the advantage. While Becker — studied him, Slade was as intently studying the engineer, prob-ing for a possible hidden weakness, the weakness that was almost always present in the outlaw, for Howard Becker was an outlaw, no different from others of the brand in the final analysis.

Despite the hazard involved, Slade admitted to himself that he enjoyed the battle of wits between them. It was exhilarating to engage a man of such out-standing ability in such a conflict. And it was up to him to make good what Captain Jim McNeity often said, that Wait Slade not only out-fought the outlaws, he out-thought them.

Grading, levelling, embanking, the rail-head boomed toward Hamon, now only a couple of miles distant, the cowboy and farmer guard pacing their horses beside the advancing steel. Work trains rumbled back and forth from the Oresta yards loaded with rails, crossties, fish plates and other materials, keeping the toilers constantly supplied with all that was needed. The camp and cook cars kept pace. Men ate standing, slept when utter exhaustion overcame them. Walt Slade kept in constant touch with developments, via telegraph, and learned that the M.K. was building north at a fast gait. It was a race, all right, and any major delay would mean the loss of the race for the C. & P. He talked with the trackmen and they redoubled their efforts.

'Drill, ye tarriers, drill!' bellowed big Terry Mulligan, the head foreman. 'Make the dirt fly! Move, you snails! Do you want to get beaten?'

Already the survey lines were being run west of Hamon with everything in readiness for the advancing steel. And the New Mexico state line was now fairly close.

This caused Slade to send a cryptic message to Captain Jim McNelty, a message that caused the telegraph operator to stare for it consisted of but two words — New Mexico.

'Is that all, Mr. Slade?' he asked.

'That's all,' Slade replied. 'You should have an answer by nightfall. Hold it for me, and — forget both messages.'
'Okay, Mr. Slade, I done forgot already,' grinned the operator as he cut in his key

and began clicking out the seemingly meaningless message.

He was even more bewildered at the answer, which was longer, consisting of *three* words — Know the governor.

Slade smiled and chuckled and left the office, the operator shaking his head and staring after him.

But *El Halcón* understood; he had all the authority he needed to cross the state line.

17

'I hardly ever get to see you anymore!' Gypsy Carvel wailed when he dropped in later that evening. 'Darn that railroad! I don't favor it, anyhow. My mother did all right with a stage coach.'

'A railroad *could* bring me back to you faster,' he pointed out.

'Which would help, if you ever decide to come back, once you're gone.'

'Make the attraction strong enough, that's up to you,' he said, crinkling his eyes at her.

'If I don't, it's from lack of opportunity,' she retorted. Sheriff Orton dropped in while Slade was eating his dinner. 'Everything quiet hereabouts,' he reported. 'How is it out on the road?'

'I have a sort of feeling that things are too darn quiet,' Slade replied. 'The work is going along at a good pace, everybody's happy and at the rate we're pushing the steel, we should win the race. That is if nothing happens to delay us. But I have a strong hunch that something is due to happen soon. May sound nonsensical, but I can't help it.'

'You and your hunches!' growled the sheriff. 'Trouble is they usually work out. Becker behaving himself?'

'Perfectly, and that's got me bothered, too. To look at him you'd say butter wouldn't melt in his mouth, to employ an old and trite saying. But it seems to me he wears the smug and demure expression of a cat that sees the canary's cage door unhooked and is just waiting to spring. I've been beating my brains out trying to anticipate his move, whatever it is, and so far with no success. He's a smooth article, all right, and has the ability, not exactly usual with the outlaw brand, to wait patiently for opportunity, the opportunity he is very likely making. And all I can do is mark time and keep my eyes open.'

'You'd better keep 'em open,' advised Orton. 'For in my opinion the move he'll make will be a move to get rid of you.'

'Could be,' Slade conceded carelessly. 'Well, we'll see.'

The sheriff grunted and ordered a snort to lay a proper foundation before eating.

'I'll bet a hatful of pesos you beat his bunch to Randal,' he observed.

'That is possible, but it doesn't solve my problem,' Slade replied. 'In fact, if we do win the race to Randal and Becker doesn't commit any further overt acts, he leaves my chore hanging in the air. For as you know, I am not here to build a railroad but to apprehend a person or persons who have broken Texas laws. Until that is done, Becker and his bunch are very much unfinished business. And if nothing happens between here and Randal, the rest of the bunch will very likely scatter and Becker can walk out thumbing his nose at me, figuratively speaking.'

'He'll end up with his blasted nose very much out of joint,' the sheriff growled. 'I'll bet on that, too.'

'Don't go overboard,' Slade laughed.

'But,' he added seriously, 'I haven't altered my opinion that *amigo* Becker will cut loose some way before we reach Randal and perhaps give me a chance to drop my loop. Here's hoping.'

Gypsy came from the back room where she had been working and joined them.

'Some new faces here tonight,' she remarked. 'Those three men at the corner table by the dance-floor, I never saw them before.'

Slade had already noticed the three men in question, quiet, alert looking individuals. All three were of medium height and build. One was very swarthy, looking almost Mexican, he thought, though possibly just with a good deal of Indian blood. They appeared to be taking everything in and more than once he had seen eyes glint in his direction. And gradually he became slightly interested in the trio.

There was nothing outstanding about any of them. They wore range-land clothes, packed guns, and their complexions bespoke an outdoor life. Very likely just visiting cowhands from some outlying spread who were in town for a mite of celebration.

But little by little he began to wonder a trifle; the three men were undoubtedly paying him more than casual attention, and there was an air of expectancy about them — as if they were waiting for something, something of which they were not quite sure.

What? He didn't know, but anything out of the ordinary interested *El Halcón*. Well, he'd wait and see. Not that he expected anything to happen in the busy saloon. Abruptly he made up his mind to something. Here might be the opportunity he was hoping for.

Gypsy was chattering away about numerous things. He answered her questions automatically and intelligently, although his mind was really elsewhere.

'Got to get back to work,' she finally said. 'Be seeing you in a little while.' She entered the back room and closed the door.

Sheriff Orton shoved his empty glass aside and glanced at the clock. He regarded the glass a moment, then apparently decided to leave it empty.

'Guess I'd better amble around a bit,' he said. 'Looks like it's going to be another big night. Going to stick around for a while?'

'For a while,' Slade replied. 'I'll very likely be here when you get back.' Orton waved his hand and departed.

Rolling a cigarette, Slade settled back comfortably in his chair. Without appearing to do so, he watched the three men at the corner table. Their heads had drawn together in low voiced conversation, and again he was sure that they glanced in his direction. Not much finesse to their mode of operating; if they really had something in mind, they had given away their intention. At least to the eyes and the instant understanding of *El Halcón*.

Abruptly he stood up and, without a glance at the corner table, walked out. But reflected in the bar mirror, he saw the three men rise to their feet.

Walking neither fast nor slow, *El Halcón* headed west toward the more questionable section of the town. Soon the lights were fewer, pedestrians less frequent. Across the street were closed warehouses and shops, their dark window glass providing a very good substitute for mirrors. And in those 'mirrors' Slade saw the three men pacing along behind him, still some little distance to the rear.

Slade knew exactly where he was going. He knew the street well and knew it would provide excellent opportunities for a drygulching, if that was what the devils had in mind. He had little fear that they would all three quicken their pace and close in on him from the rear. Not even they, in expert stalkers as they were, would make such a rash move. It would be something a bit more clever than that.

Now the street was deserted with only the glow from dingy saloon windows casting shadowy gleams of light across the board sidewalk. Slade watched the reflections in the windows across the street, saw one of them slither around a corner and out of sight. And now he knew just what to expect and how the business was planned. The plan was to catch him between a deadly cross-fire. Might have worked with a less wary and experienced individual. As it was, Slade was quite pleased by the development. Knowing the street as he did, he also knew just what to do. Looked like a chance to possibly take one of the hellions alive and persuade him to do a little talking.

Directly ahead, less than half a block away was the mouth of a dark alley that ran between rows of warehouses to the next street south. Glancing across the street, Slade saw that the two men were closing the distance.

Suddenly he bounded ahead, raced at top speed toward the alley. Behind him sounded a curse. But before the two pursuers, thrown off balance by the unexpectedness of the move, could recover, Slade bad reached the alley mouth. Still going at top speed he swerved into it, ducking and dodging. There was a startled yelp. A man loomed in front of him. Slade's keen eyes caught the gleam of the gun he held. He drew and shot with both hands a split second before the other pulled trigger. The slug whisked past his face. The gunman gave a gasping cry and fell.

Slade whirled to face the alley mouth. The other two members of the unsavory trio bulged into view, guns blazing toward the swerving, weaving, shadowy form of the Ranger. Both Slade's Colts let go with a rattling roar.

One of the men went backward as if struck by a mighty fist, fairly lifted off his feet by the forty-five slugs that hammered his body. His companion lurched, reeled, and went down soddenly. A single glance told Slade there was nothing more to be feared from either one of them. He turned toward the moaning, gurgling wretch on the ground almost beside him.

The fellow was still alive, but he was going fast, his life draining out through his shattered lungs. Slade holstered his guns and knelt beside him. It was the swarthy member of the trio. Glazing eyes filled with terror met his.

Slade spoke, his voice calm, dispassionate.

'Why not lighten the load a little before you take the big jump?' he said, repeating the words in Spanish, which he had a feeling the dying man understood better than English. 'Come clean, now. Who paid you to try and kill me, and what will be the next move?'

The quiet confident voice seemed to light a spark of hope in the agonized eyes, the eyes of a man who was looking across into eternity and seeing it wasn't far. His blood-frothed lips moved. A word gurgled forth, '*Cabeza!*'

Spanish for head. Doubtless the poor devil's head was bursting with fever. As Slade Jeaned close, he repeated the word, gaspingly. 'Cabeza — ca — ca — '

Blood gushed from his mouth, drowning the incompleted word in a red flood. His chest arched mightily as he fought for air. It sank in, and did not rise again.

With a sigh, Slade straightened up. So blasted close! But not close enough. What looked like a promising lead went aglimmering with the departing soul.

18

Voices were sounding not far off. Soon somebody would come prowling around to try and learn what the shooting was about, and Slade was in no mood to explain. He passed swiftly down the alley to the far street and turned back toward Gypsy Carvel's saloon. Doubtless someone would notify the sheriff, if he hadn't already heard the shooting, and Orton wouldn't waste much time contacting the Ranger.

Well, one thing was sure for certain. Howard Becker was not thoroughly familiar with *El Halcón's* reputation. The latest attempt hadn't been quite as clumsy as the one by the stable in the alley, but anyone really acquainted with The Hawk would have known darn well it wouldn't work. Perhaps, though, it would prove to be the last try. Becker's bunch must be pretty well cleared out.

Not that the cunning devil would give

up so easily. Slade still believed he had an ace in the hole that be would play when the time was ripe. Against that he must make every possible provision.

The great drawback relative to that laudable determination lay in the fact he hadn't the slightest idea what to provide against. With a shrug of his shoulders, he turned a corner and a few minutes later entered the saloon.

Gypsy was at the table she held reserved for him. 'Walt where have you been? Getting into trouble, I'll warrant,' she greeted him accusingly.

'Just taking a little walk,' he replied cheerfully. 'How about some coffee?'

They were having the coffee together when Sheriff Orton walked in, rather hurriedly. He *looked* accusingly at Slade although he asked no questions until Gypsy had departed to attend to some chores. Then, resignedly, 'Okay, let's have it.' Slade told him. 'I thought for a minute I'd struck paydirt,' he concluded. 'The fellow was afraid to die and wanted to ease his conscience before cashing in, of that I'm positive.

He was all set to answer any questions I might ask him, but he didn't last long enough.'

'Sometimes I'd say you shoot too darn straight, that is if it wasn't fairly important that you stay alive,' the sheriff grunted.

'Well, I didn't exactly have time to pick my spots,' Slade replied. 'That sidewinder had an iron in his hand and was all ready for business when I barged into the alley. If he hadn't been thrown off balance for a second by what he didn't expect happening, the end might have been different. And the other two weren't throwing spit balls at me. They were just a mite too excited and blundered right in front of me, shooting in every direction and not taking time to line sights.'

'Oh, sure, just as easy as all that!' snorted Orton. 'I kinda get to believing you're part cat, not only on your feet but with nine lives, corralled, too. How many you got left?'

'One, at least, so far,' Slade smiled.

The sheriff did not look convinced.

'I had some fellers pack the carcasses to the office,' he said. 'Like to look 'em over?'

'Yes, I would,' Slade answered. 'Let's go; Gypsy's busy and won't have time to throw a tantrum. I believe she's beginning to think you are a bad influence.'

'She'll get over it,' said the sheriff. 'Come along.'

In the office, Slade gave the bodies a careful once-over, and learned nothing.

'Border scum again,' was his verdict. 'The sort that would poison their own grandmothers were the price right. Would do anything for money, and quite probably Becker has a very nice drawing account.'

'Do you think those railroad folks would stand for the things he's been doing?' the sheriff asked curiously.

'Frankly, I doubt it,' Slade answered. 'But I fear they are somewhat in the position of the fellow who got the bear by the tail and would have liked to let go but couldn't. Becker is shrewd and managed to sell himself and his scheme to them. There are ways to slow construction without risking murder, and, after all, he hasn't killed anybody with his shenanigans, so far. And were he locked up for the things he's done, he knows they would move heaven and earth going to bat for him so he wouldn't talk. That is, they'd think he wouldn't. More likely he would talk if he felt it was to his interest to do so. He's for Becker, first, last, and always.'

'He's tried to have you killed,' the sheriff pointed out.

'Yes,' Slade conceded, 'but remember he looks on me as one of his own brand, an owlhoot trying to horn in and skim off the cream. He probably believes you have brought me in to do your gunning for him. Some peace officers *have* been known to do that, you know. Look what happened up in the panhandle a few years back.'

'Guess you're right,' Orton agreed, 'but it puts you on one heck of a spot.'

'Nothing bad happened so far,' Slade said cheerfully. He gazed at the stark forms on the floor.

'The small dark one is the one I'd hoped would talk,' he observed. 'I feel pretty sure he was a Mexican. Seemed to understand perfectly when I spoke to him in Spanish, and tried to answer in the same language. Nothing in their pockets of any interest, I see. I expect you'll find their horses around somewhere and can dispose of them; more *dinero* for your treasury.'

'You should take a cut,' said the sheriff. 'Because of you the county is getting rich. Now what?'

'Might as well get back to Gypsy,' Slade decided. 'Tomorrow I'll have to amble to the railhead again. Might as well. Seems all I do in town is get shot at.'

'I'd say you're doing a good chore of ridding the land of some pests,' observed Orton. 'And I guarantee there'll be less widelooping and holdups in the section for a while.'

Gypsy heaved a sigh of relief when they put in an appearance.

'I was just wondering,' she said. 'The boys are buzzing about a shooting over to the west of here. Seems three men shot each other down. Nobody seems to know why.'

'That wasn't nice of them,' Slade remarked. Gypsy gave him a searching look but refrained from asking questions.

'And I'm going to bed,' the sheriff announced. 'Old bones need their rest.' He ambled out.

Gypsy regarded Slade through her lashes, and glanced at the clock.

* * *

Without interruption, the railhead rolled on to Hamon to the accompaniment of clashing steel, thudding hammers and booming dynamite. Slade was highly pleased with the progress made. And Howard Becker seemed pleased about something, for an occasional smile twitched his gray lips and there was an amused expression in his dark eyes.

Which gave Walt Slade a feeling of

disquietude. What *did* Becker have up his sleeve!

Word had come that the M.K. was having trouble with a rough terrain but nevertheless was forging ahead at a fast pace. It was a tight race, with little needed to turn the balance one way or another.

Now Slade rode well ahead of the survey line, probing, studying, estimating what grading and what embankment would be necessary. Summing up difficulties, endeavoring to ascertain the best method of overcoming them, visioning the railroad line as it would be when completed, he was constantly trying to choose the best route to Randal. He shook his head as he surveyed a bristling and craggy spur of the Tonto Hills that extended its ominous length across his path. There was no circumventing the range; the road must cross it.

'Horse,' he said to Shadow, 'I know a crack through those hunks of rock. Rode it once and as I recall it wasn't too bad. Of course then I was not considering it as a pass for a railroad, which is different from ambling along with you, just going somewhere and taking a short cut. It will be a short cut for the steel if we can make it through. Well, we'll go see.'

Shadow offered no objections and moseyed on; anything to please his loco master.

With the plainsman's unerring instinct for distance and direction, Slade rode straight to the canyon's mouth, eyeing its stern portals which were of adamantine stone.

Crack just about described it, for it was very narrow and in places the cliffs overhung, so that it was shadowy. Only the dregs of light managed to seep to its depths. The cliffs were tall but unbroken, no cracks, no fissures, and gave the appearance of being as solid as when terrestrial convulsions raised them from the surrounding plain.

'Doesn't look like we would be bothered much by rock falls in the course of the spring thaws,' he remarked to the horse. 'Which is a decided advantage; won't be plagued by them as they are in

Cajun and other passes. No, it doesn't appear too bad.'

Along the south wall ran a slow, deep stream of sullen water that gushed unexpectedly from the cliff. However, the bank was rather high and he visioned little danger from flood water.

Considerable grading would be required and the rock which formed the floor of the gorge would be hard to move. Plenty of dynamite would take care of that, though, and as he rode, Slade became convinced that the cleft provided a reasonable passage through the hills.

The canyon was something more than three miles long and very nearly straight, opening onto level rangeland beyond that continued to Randal and would intrude no serious obstacles.

'Yes, horse, this will do,' he said. 'The trains will go through here a-whoopin'. A lot better than having to cut our way through the hills with grades so steep that they would slow up traffic badly. Yep, we'll run the survey lines right through, and the steel is walking right after the surveyors; the boys are sure bending their back and making the dirt fly. Old Man Dunn will be pleased when be gets back from Chicago. Heard from him this morning, by wire. Says he may have to go to New York for a spell and then back to Chicago for another short spell. He's got some sort of a big deal, a merger, I think, on his hands. I know he has his eye on a certain eastern road and has for some time. I've a notion he'll put it over. Well, we're doing our part over here. That is, so far as building a railroad is concerned. But I wasn't sent here to build a railroad, and so far as what I came for, I seem to be getting exactly nowhere. Blast it! Why couldn't that hellion who tried to drygulch me in the alley have lived long enough to do a little talking. He was all set to, on that I'll bet a handful of pesos. Well, he didn't last long enough and there's no sense in crying over spilt milk, or spilt blood as was the case in that instance.'

Shadow had listened patiently to the foregoing harangue and now he snorted relief as Slade turned his head and rode back to Hamon.

19

Hard on the heels of the railhead, a long string of camp cars loaded with workers rolled into Hamon. There was a station and a freight house to be built, well-planned, substantial structures, and sidings and loading pens. Jaggers Dunn did nothing by half and the C. & P. was famous for its consideration of its patrons. All possible conveniences would be provided.

And with the advent of the work crews, Hamon had quite a celebration. No liquor was sold in Hamon, but from some mysterious source bottles appeared, plenty of them, from which railroaders and farmers imbibed liquid refreshment in large enough quantities to insure a high old time for all hands.

After a day and a night of hilarity, the crews buckled down to work and worked with a will. The construction was moving along smoothly at a pace that satisfied

Slade.

But all was not peace and tranquillity elsewhere. Complaints of stolen cattle were coming in from the northern and the southwestern ranches. Never big herds, but enough in small bunches to give the owners concern.

'What do you make of it?' Sheriff Orton asked Slade. More widelooping in the past month than there's been in a year.'

'I would say,' Slade replied, 'that while Becker has gotten completely out of control where the M.K. is concerned, the hellions he brought in with him, what's left of them, have gotten completely out of control where he is concerned and are going it on their own. To hold his men in check, an outlaw leader has to keep them plentifully supplied with ready cash and I'm of the opinion there is a limit to how much money Becker can put out. That, I believe, is the answer.'

'And more trouble,' growled the sheriff. 'Pears to be no end to it.'

'But it could work to our advantage,'

Slade said thoughtfully. 'If the devils are on the loose, they'll lack Becker's guiding brain and may make a slip that will provide us with opportunity.'

'I hope so,' the sheriff replied wearily.

A couple of days later, Bije Manning, the keeper of the general store, relayed a bit of information that evoked in Slade a feeling of disquietude.

'Don't know who started it or how or where,' said Manning, 'but there's a whisper going around that there are some mean and ornery scuts among the railroad builders and that they plan to do something bad here in town before long. I personally don't believe it, but there are quite a few folks who are doing a mite of wondering. Figured you should know about it.'

'Thanks, Bije, I'm very glad you told me,' Slade answered. 'Looks like somebody is trying to deliberately stir up trouble.'

'That's the way I figure it,' nodded Manning. 'But what I can't figure is who is back of it.'

Slade had a very good notion as to who was back of it. His problem was to endeavor to thwart whatever Becker had in mind, for there was little doubt in his mind but that the cunning devil would make good on his whispering campaign and put the railroad workers in a bad light if he wasn't stopped. And it was up to *El Halcón* to stop him or to make the attempt abortive. He cudgeled his brains in a painstaking effort to anticipate what Becker had in mind.

A drygulching of some prominent citizen of Hamon? No, that would not be effective. A drygulching cannot be accomplished in the presence of witnesses and if somebody was shot down from ambush it would be impossible to pin the crime on the railroaders, which must be done were Becker to accomplish his purpose.

No, it would be something subtle, out of the ordinary, ingenious, carefully planned and executed. Something that would definitely pin the act on the railroad builders. But how in blazes was that to be done!

One by one, Slade conned over every possible strike Becker might make. There was no bank in Hamon but it was well known that Manning's store functioned as one, to all practical purposes. There was always plenty of money in his old iron strongbox, which stood in the rear room of the store. And that old box would offer little difficulty to even the most amateurish safe cracker.

Yes, a try for that *dinero* might well be in the cards. Quite logical were it but a band of regulation owlhoots out for gain. But again, how in blazes would it benefit Becker and his schemes to allow the M. K. to forge ahead of the C. & P. in the railroad building race! To rob Manning's safe would require secrecy and an opportunity after nightfall. That was the only reasonable viewpoint. The robbers, if such a depredation were planned, could hardly run down the street waving their loot and then take refuge in the camp cars.

Well, the war of wits must go on, with

Becker, seemingly, always a jump ahead. Slade planned his own campaign with care and meticulous regard for details.

A couple of details, incidentally, he believed were in his favor. Namely, that Becker considered him either just Jaggers Dunn's trouble shooter called in to handle difficult chores, or *El Halcón*, another owlhoot with designs on his, Becker's, preserves. He still believed that Becker hadn't the least notion that he was a Texas Ranger, and because of which he might possibly grow a mite careless.

Every day Slade rode the course of the track laying and the survey line that was fast approaching the canyon pass through the hills, but each night found him back in Hamon. Around nine o'clock he would retire to Bije Manning's residence, presumably for the night. He would sleep between two and three hours and shortly after midnight, when the town was growing quiet, he would slip out the back way and by a circuitous route reach a point near the back of Manning's store, where he would take his post and await developments.

They were slow in coming, and after the fourth night of tiresome vigil, he began to wonder uneasily if his hunch was a straight one. Perhaps Becker had something entirely different in mind and would put it into action while he, Slade, whiled away the tedious hours keeping watch on the general store.

The fifth night promised an even more uncomfortable period of guard duty for there was a hint of rain. When Slade left Bije Manning's house, a mist was already in the air and with it was an unpleasant chill. With little hope of better luck, he drew near the store. Then abruptly he halted, straining his eyes.

From where he stood he could view the barred window of the back room. Each previous night that window had been a black square of darkness; but tonight it showed a faint glow, little more than what might arise from a heap of fungus or even a decaying animal, but a glow that the keen vision of *El Halcón* instantly spotted.

Careful not to make the slightest sound, Slade stole forward. The store backed onto an alley where there were no street lights, so the misty glow would not be a window pane reflection.

Slow step by slow step, he approached the building which loomed gaunt against the overcast sky. Once he paused for moments when a slight sound from down the alley reached his ears, a sound like the impatient pawing of a horse. However, it was not repeated and he resumed his stealthy advance.

Without mishap he reached the rear wall of the store and edged along it toward the window. Another moment and he was able to peer through; he breathed an exultant exclamation.

Inside the back room a light burned, a dim light, like that cast by a bull's-eye lantern with the shade partially closed. Another instant and he could make out the figures of two men who knelt before the old iron strongbox, busy with something that in the faint glow he could not quite make out for sure.

One thing *was* sure for certain, though. No doubt but they were opening the safe. He debated a moment whether he should smash the window pane with a gun barrel, cover them, and call upon them to surrender. Then he recalled that a little way along the side of the building was a door, presumably locked, by way of which the pair had very likely gained entrance, Better to slip in the door and corner them in the back room, which he believed he could easily do. He straightened up, started to turn, then halted.

Beside the strongbox a tiny flame had leaped into being, the flame of a lighted match. Instantly it was followed by a rain of sparks. The hellions were blowing the safe! He saw the two men rear up and turn to run back from the coming explosion.

There was a blinding flash, a deafening roar. Slade was showered with broken glass and hurled clean off his feet by the blast of displaced air howling through the shattered window. The dynamite or

242

nitroglycerin or whatever the devil it was had cut loose prematurely.

Picking himself up, thankful that he had escaped with but a few minor scratches from the flying window glass, Slade made his way to the side door. He knew well there was no hurry; the two safecrackers had caught the full force of the blast and couldn't possibly have survived it.

As he expected, the door stood ajar. He pushed it wide open and entered. The room was full of smoke which he recognized as nitroglycerin fumes, but there was no sign of fire.

Being familiar with the layout of the store, he groped his way to a bracket lamp and touched a match to the wick. A little farther back was a second lamp which he also lighted. Its glow penetrated the back room.

In there fumes were thick, the breathing none too good. However, that would be adjusted quickly as misty air poured in through the broken window. Slade leaned against the wall and rolled a cigarette.

Shouts were sounding, and a babble of voices was swiftly drawing nearer. Another moment and men bulged in through the open door, halted and stood staring at the tall Ranger puffing nonchalantly on his cigarette.

'Send somebody to fetch Manning,' Stade directed. 'The rest of you come in back with me. Something to show you. It won't be nice seeing, but you'd better have a look at it.' With the crowd, constantly augmented by new arrivals, muttering after him, he led the way to the back room, the second bracket lamp in his hand.

'Come on,' he told the farmers who hung back. 'Come on, they won't hurt you, or anybody else from now on.'

The crowd edged forward gingerly and peered into the still smoky back room. Then they halted as if they had run into a stone wall to stand staring.

The safe door had been blown from its hinges and was imbedded in the far wall. But the inner compartments of the safe, though somewhat splintered, were still closed. A little way back from the safe lay the mangled bodies of the safe crackers, their faces ripped and shredded beyond human semblance.

'They did a pretty good chore of opening the safe, blowing out windows, and bringing down plaster from the ceiling, but the explosion was just a mite premature,' Slade told his dumfounded audience. 'All right, wait until Manning gets here before touching anything.'

Manning arrived very shortly, in a state of half-dress, his eyes wild and staring.

'Slade!' he exclaimed. 'What in tophet happened?'

'Sorry I got here a mite too late to save your safe door and the ceiling,' Slade replied. 'Otherwise, though, I think you'll find everything intact. All right, let's have a closer look at those carcasses.'

They entered the room and squatted beside the bodies.

They were clothed in greasy overalls and jumpers and on their feet were the heavy, high-laced shoes favored by the railroad construction workers.

The farmers leaned close staring at that tell-tale garb.

Glancing up, Slade saw their faces had set like stone. He smiled a trifle.

Surprisingly, the hands of one of the dead men had completely escaped injury. Slade turned the palms up and examined them closely.

'Bije,' he said, 'take a look at this.' He turned to the crowd.

'Any of you fellows at all familiar with the cattle husiness?' he asked. 'If so, come forward.'

Several men immediately shoved to the front. Silently, Slade pointed at the turned-up palms. The farmers peered close, muttered under their breadth. It was Bije Manning, who had handled cattle before coming to west Texas, who broke the silence.

'Yep, Walt, you're right, per usual. The skunk never got those scars and calluses from pick and shovel. Those are rope and branding iron marks. Right, fellers?' The others nodded sober agreement.

'But what in creation does it mean?' demanded one bewildered old-timer. 'Why are they wearin' those railroad worker duds?'

Slade stood up and let the full force of his steady eyes rest on the gathering.

'It means,' he said quietly, 'that somebody is deliberately trying to stir up trouble between you folks and the railroad boys. Do you understand? Look down the alley a ways, and I think you'll find a couple of saddled and bridled horses hitched to something. And I'll wager their rig is rangeland.' He did not tell them the grim conclusion at which he had arrived relative to the happening. And the farmers were too excited and too ready to accept his explanation to argue or ask questions.

While they chattered and gestured, Slade took the lamp and searched the room, Manning tagging along. Finally he stooped and picked up something with an exclamation of satisfaction.

'Thought maybe I would find it,' he told his companion. 'I sure hoped I would, for it confirms the decision I had already reached.'

'What is it?' Manning asked. 'Looks like a bit of fuse.'

'That's just what it is,' Slade replied in tones too low for the others to catch. 'It's a piece of the fuse used to detonate the cap and set off the nitroglycerin. But it is not ordinary fuse. It is a quick-burning fuse, the kind sometimes used in the course of drilling a gas well. The fire, when it was lighted, instead of sputtering along, raced down the fuse to the cap and exploded the nitro before that pair could get in the clear. And listen, Bije, don't mention this to anybody; I'll explain why later.'

'Certain,' muttered Manning. 'Now what?'

'Now we hang something over that window to keep out the cold air and the wet. Leave everything else just as is; I want the sheriff to see it before it is touched. Then I'm going to the telegraph shanty to send Orton a wire. The operator will be off duty but I can handle the key. You'd better lock up and go to bed.'

'I'll go with you to send the wire,' Manning offered. 'I couldn't sleep now, anyway.'

'Okay,' Slade agreed.

At that juncture a man rushed in to report the finding of the safe crackers' horses and that the rig was rangeland. Which did not at all surprise Slade.

'Stable them for the sheriff,' he directed. A heavy blanket from the stock was quickly tacked over the shattered window, the crowd was shooed out, and Manning locked the door.

'Wonder how the devils got in — they didn't bust the lock,' Manning remarked.

'Key made from a wax impression, the chances are,' Slade explained. 'No trouble if you know how.' Manning nodded his understanding.

'You said you'd tell me what you meant about that piece of fuse,' Manning suggested as they headed for the telegraph shanty.

'It meant,' Slade replied grimly,

'that the killing of that pair was coldly calculated, snake-blooded murder. The man who provided the nitre and the fuse knew exactly what he was doing. He knew that whoever lighted that fuse would be killed by the resulting explosion, almost certainly both would die.'

'But why did he do it?' Manning asked in puzzled tones. 'Bije, can't you see it?' Slade answered. 'Wasn't the crowd instantly certain that the railroad workers were responsible for what happened tonight?'

'Yes,' Manning admitted, 'and if you hadn't showed them they were wrong, they'd still be certain.'

'Exactly,' Slade said. 'And if something really bad happened to the construction work, what would be the natural conclusion on the part of everybody?'

'That the farmers did it to get even,' Manning instantly answered.

'Yes, in retaliation for what happened tonight, with suspicion directed away from the man really responsible.'

250

'I can see it now, after you showed me,' Manning admitted. 'That scoundrel, whoever he is, is worse than a mad dog. Walt, do you know who he is?'

'I do, but unfortunately I can't prove it,' Slade replied. 'I can't prove anything against him, yet. Now, however, there's a charge against him that will cause him to stretch rope, if brought to court.'

'He'll stretch it, all right, if he don't eat lead first,' Manning declared confidently. 'Well, here's the shanty.'

Opening the shack with a key he carried, Slade quickly tapped out a message to Sheriff Orton, ordering the Cresta operator to deliver it at once.

'Old Brad will be here shortly after daylight, you can depend on that,' Slade told his companion as he locked the shanty. 'Now I'm going to try and get a little rest; haven't slept much the past week.'

'So you been keeping tabs on the store all week, eh?'

'Yes, for the past five nights,' Slade admitted. 'Playing a hunch, as it were, that if something was pulled it would most likely be there.' He did not bother to explain that the hunch was based on sound reasoning and deduction.

20

Sheriff Orton arrived early and he and Slade immediately went into conference.

'So after all we've got a real killer on our hands, eh?' he remarked when Slade concluded his recital of the night's events.

'Yes,' the Ranger replied. 'A cold, calculating, utterly callous one. He sacrificed those poor devils to his own expedience. I've about arrived at the conclusion that he has a hard core of ruthless hellions be brought here with him, men he trusts and whom he can depend on to play the game his way. Very likely he has recruited some border scum, such as we have remarked on, to handle small chores and he considers them strictly expendable. They, incidentally, are in my opinion the wideloopers who have started operating in this section.'

'But just what did he hope to gain by last night's performance?' the sheriff wondered.

'I've thought that out and have concluded that it was primarily for the purpose of distracting attention from his main project, whatever the devil that is. With suspicion generated between the workers and the farmers, everybody would be concentrating on that angle.'

'And if it wasn't for you convincing the farmers that the railroaders had nothing to do with what happened, he'd have gotten away with it,' Orton commented.

'Quite likely,' Slade admitted. 'Well, he didn't, but he's got some sort of an ace he aims to play at just the right time, on that you can depend. Well, a small pair beats an ace, so perhaps we'll come out on top before all is said and done. Now suppose we drop over to the store so you can have a look-see. I told Manning to leave everything just as it was.'

In the wrecked rear room, Orton looked things over and swore whole-heartedly.

'It's a mess,' he growled. 'A wonder they didn't blow up the whole store.'

'They probably would have, had they

not handled the stuff rather expertly,' Slade explained. He gestured to a hand drill lying against the far wall.

'They drilled holes, poured the soup in between the outer and inner skins of the door, evidently pouring it carefully to the last drop so there was no residue sitting around to cut loose when the blast when off. That way the safe absorbed most of the shock of the blast. They over-estimated the charge a bit, though, and smashed the window and brought down a portion of the ceiling. However, had the fuse been of the conventional type they would have had time to get in the clear before the explosion, and had. they not been interrupted, they would have cleaned the safe and high-tailed. That, however, is just what the head devil didn't want to happen; he wanted the bodies to be found here at the scene of the blast.'

He paused to roll a cigarette and resumed.

'I slipped a mite. I was of the opinion that nothing would be attempted until after midnight, when the streets were deserted and everything quiet. So I got here just a few minutes late. Otherwise, I might have been able to take at least one of them alive and perhaps have persuaded him to talk a little. I don't know how much they knew — perhaps they never even contacted Becker, who could have worked through an intermediary he trusted. But I *was* late, with the results you see.'

'Uh-huh, and if you'd gotten here a mite earlier and got inside and started a corpse-and-cartridge session, a stray slug might have set the stuff off and blowed you through the roof. Nitro is darned senstive, don't take much to set it off.'

Slade did not argue the point, for there was truth in what the sheriff said.

It was a rather grisly task, but Sheriff Orton examined the contents of the dead men's pockets, and turned up nothing significant. The horses they had left hitched in the alley were also examined. Their brands proved to be meaningless skillet of-snakes Mexican burns. They

256

were good critters and the sheriff turned them over to Bije Manning.

'What they'll bring will pay part of the damage done to your joint' he told the storekeeper.

The local doctor, who also acted as undertaker, was summoned and the bodies carted away. After which Manning began repairs on his back room and his safe.

'What you figure to do?' Orton asked of Slade.

'I'm going to head back to Oresta with you,' the Ranger decided. 'Gypsy will think I've plumb deserted her a little early in the game. Then I'll start riding the survey line again and try and figure what that sidewinder has planned. I'll guarantee it will be a lulu, whatever it is.'

'Much farther to go?'

'Not a great deal,' Slade answered. 'The grading and the steel are well into that narrow canyon, almost half way through it, in fact, with no major difficulties encountered. Then it will be a straight and easy shoot across the level range to Randal. From what I hear, we are ahead of the M. K. at present, but any lengthy delay for us and they'll be ahead. It's still a race.'

'When they reached Oresta, Gypsy said, 'I was beginning to wonder a little, but I didn't really believe you'd go prancing off for good without seeing me first.'

★ ★ ★

The following day, Slade again headed for the survey line, which was now far beyond the west mouth of the narrow canyon that was resounding with the thudding of spike mauls and the scrape of shovels.

The workers greeted him with shouts of welcome and he paused for a while at the head of the grading, then rode on.

He was nearing the west mouth of the canyon when he saw a horseman approaching. It turned out to be an elderly rancher who owned a spread to the west and north. They drew rein together.

'Reckon you're the young feller in charge of the railroad building, ain't you?' said the oldster. 'Folks over at Hamon were talking about you and mentioned what you look like.'

'Guess you're near enough right to get by,' Slade admitted, with a smile.

'Ain't you scairt to build through Skull Canyon?' the other remarked jocularly. 'The Mexicans, and some old-timers who should know better, will tell you it's haunted.'

'Skull Canyon!' Slade repeated.

'That's right,' nodded the rancher. 'Used to be heaps of skulls in it; the Indians fought battles here. Skull Canyon.' Abruptly the concentration furrow deepened between Slade's black brows and he hardly heard the other's next remark. For in his ears sounded the voice of a dying man, gurgling through the blood that choked his throat — 'Cabeza — ca — ca — '

So that was what the poor devil was trying to reply when *El Halcón* asked him where the next move would be made *Cabeza Cañon!*

Trying to ease his conscience and make his load into the hereafter lighter.

Craneo was the precise Spanish for skull, but illiterate Mexicans often employed the better known *cabeza* to designate either head or skull.

Skull Canyon! Where the next move would be made, doubtless the last, were it successful. Slade was convinced there would be no need of another.

'I'll have to be riding,' he told the rancher. 'Go ahead and watch the work; I've a notion you'll find it interesting.' 'I was figuring to do that,' said the other. 'Be seeing you.' They parted company, Slade beating his brains out in an endeavor to solve the riddle posed by the dying drygulcher's last words.

'Feller,' he murmured, apropos of the drygulcher, 'somehow I've a notion that when you stand up to the last tally, what you told me is going to react in your favor. I hope so. *Gracias, amigo!*'

As he rode, Slade studied the faces of

the cliffs. Here the overhang to the south was wide and massive, extending beyond the stream that washed the south cliff base almost to the middle of the canyon. But to all appearances it was utterly solid, no cracks or fissures, an unbroken surface of dark stone. No, that couldn't be it. But what in blazes *could* it be! Well out onto the level rangeland he rode, the concentration furrow deep between his black brows, thinking, thinking! Trying to analyze the situation as it stood. Trying to put himself in Becker's place, to think as he thought, to act as he might be supposed to act.

For he had a dread presentiment that there was very little time at his disposal. Did he not quickly arrive at a correct conclusion, he feared there was every chance that the construction work would be halted indefinitely and, which from his Ranger point of view was even more important, Howard Becker would go free.

After a while he drew rein and sat gazing back at the grim spoils of that ominous crack through the rugged hills. The cliffs, gleaming in the sunlight, seemed to leer derisively, mocking him, defying him to read aright their closely guarded secret. They appeared imbued with malevolent life, straining toward him, striving to free themselves from the eternal stone on which they were based and hurl their adamantine might at this human atom that sought to pit his puny strength against their colossal force.

For some little time *El Halcón* sat brooding, still gazing at those sneering cliffs. His glance roved over the prairie, deserted for as far as even his extraordinary vision could reach, then swung back again to the barriers of stone that exuded a nameless threat.

Abruptly he had an inspiration.

'I'll show you!' he muttered and turned Shadow's nose south.

At a fast pace he rode until the hills began to peter out. He turned east and rode in the shadow of their crags. After considerable searching he found a slope the black horse could negotiate and after a hard struggle with thorny brush and loose stones reached the crest with Shadow in a thoroughly disgusted frame of mind.

It took more than an hour to cross the broken and ragged crest, but finally he reached the lip of the canyon and gazed into its depths. Moving back where the going was better he continued west until he knew he was nearing the ominous overhang which was his goal. Abruptly he pulled Shadow to a halt.

'Somehow, feller, I don't like the looks of what's ahead,' he told the horse. 'So I'm going to leave you right here for a spell. Take it easy, now.'

Dismounting, he moved to the very lip of the overhang and walked slowly, very slowly, westward. And as he walked, there grew an eerie impression that he was walking toward a rendezvous with death.

The notion was ridiculous, he told himself. He was not going to slip and fall and there was nobody within miles of him, of that he was certain. But just the same the feeling persisted, grew stronger. Each slow forward step was a step of the death walk. Ahead was something waiting, waiting, ready to spring. And overhead, a sinister black shape circled and circled. A vulture! Also waiting — waiting!

Leaning over, he gazed into the shadowy depths of the canyon. Its floor was deserted. Nothing moved save the faint ripples of the sullen stream chafing against the cliffs. He turned back to the death walk.

His glance swerved to the left and suddenly he froze motionless, his hair prickling, his palms damp.

A little more than a score of feet to the left was a fissure in the stone crest. It was but a yard or so in width and extended westward for something more than a hundred feet. And Slade instantly estimated that it sank just a few feet, perhaps only a few inches back from where the overhang joined the parent cliff.

'Blast it!' he growled. 'My weight wouldn't tip the balance — maybe!'

All right to partially reassure himself, but just the same he turned with care and walked back the way he had come, and with each retreating step, a surge of relief, of confidence welled and strengthened. And it seemed to his vivid imaginination that behind him the thing that had waited gnashed with baffled fury. And as he glanced up at the blue sky, he again felt that queer prickling at the roots of his hair. The vulture was gone!

21

It was with a deep breath of relief that he passed beyond the cleft in the crest floor. Then he circled it and approached from the far side to peer into its gloomy depths. Dropping a rock fragment into it, he waited. Several seconds passed before the sound of the rock striking bottom came back to his ears. The darn thing extended downward to the canyon floor or beyond. And as he gazed toward the lip of the overhang he saw that his estimate of where the fissure split the crest floor in relation to the junction of the overhang and the cliff was very accurate.

The overhang was, figuratively speaking, attached to the canyon wall by a mere thread of stone. A single well-placed charge of dynamite would send the overhang crashing to the canyon floor.

The result? The canyon blocked by a mass of stone it would take many days to remove. And, which was worse, the stream dammed and the whole east stretch of the gorge flooded.

The C. & P. would lose the race to Randal and, more important from Slade's point of view, Howard Becker would amble off, with nothing proven against him, to collect his stipend from the M.K. and to try a little genteel blackmail which Slade believed him shrewd enough to put across. He'd be all set for some other hellishness with murder quite likely a sideline.

'Oh, they don't often come like him, heaven be praised' Slade remarked to Shadow. 'Brains, ability, originality, and utter ruthlessness! Quite a gent! Well, we'll see.'

Squatting comfortably on his heels, he rolled and lighted a cigarette, gazing at the lip of the overhang. Ridiculous, of course, to think his added weight would topple the darn thing. Just the same he preferred not to repeat that eerie death walk unless obliged to.

Of course there was a logical explanation

for the disquieting sensations that had beset him. His steps had doubtless set up a tiny vibration in the poised overhang that had communicated to his subconscious mind. Perhaps!

Carefully pinching out the butt and casting it aside, he began a meticulous search of the crest. It did not take him long to unearth indubitable evidence that a horse or two had been tethered there no great time before.

Yes, this was it. Becker had evidently carefully explored the country west of Oresta and had concluded that the canyon might offer opportunity should other expedients fail. Giving the surroundings a careful once-over, he had hit on the fis sure and with his knowledge of engineering had instantly recognized its possibilities.

Mounting, Slade rode back down the slopes to the rangeland, and as he rode, he made his plans.

He had noted that midway along the fissure was a spot where, a couple of feet below the surface, the overhang-side showed several cracks which would accommodate the dynamite were his surmise as to Becker's intentions correct. And nearby was a jut of stone that would afford him concealment, the location of which he had carefully placed in his mind. 'And this time, feller, I'll try and not be too late,' he told the horse.

Abandoning the survey line for the time being, he rode directly to the canyon mouth and entered. As he passed under the overhang he studied it with care. It looked perfectly innocent, solid and firm as the very foundations of the world. Nevertheless he was glad when he was no longer beneath the ominous mass of stone. He rode on to the railhead where he paused a while, chatting with the track layers and graders, satisfied with the progress being made. He resolved firmly that all their loyal efforts should not be for naught.

He wondered what had caused that strange crack in the cliff. The region had once been highly volcanic, and perhaps some terrific outburst of superheated steam had riven the stone. Or, which he thought more likely, the erosive effect of wind and snow and rain over the course of untold ages had dissolved a softer strata. Either assumption was geologically sound.

Well, it didn't matter how it got there. It would have to be taken care of. Which posed no overly difficult engineering problem.

After thinking the matter over carefully from all angles, Slade concluded that if Becker really intended to act, he would do so without undue delay. The steel was fast forging ahead, with a string of camp cars poised to follow, and Becker would assuredly not want a trainload of workers tools, and materials beyond the west mouth of the canyon: these would greatly expedite the removal of the fallen stone and the draining off of the flood water. Yes, any time, now, and Slade felt he could take no chances.

'Going to mean some tough going for both of us, but I reckon we can take it,' he told Shadow who declined to express an opinion.

As a result of his decision, night after night Slade sent the black horse toiling up the rocky, brush-grown slopes to the crest and across to the lip of the canyon, where he concealed Shadow in a clump of thicket and took up his post behind the jut of stone he had previously marked.

For three nights he kept tiresome watch until not long before dawn. Nothing happened and he grew heartily weary of the affair, beginning to wonder if he was following a cold trail.

The fourth night was one of a full moon in a clear sky that flooded the wild scene with ghostly light.

It was nearing midnight when a sound broke the vast stillness of the wastelands, a sound Slade instantly recognized as the click of horses' irons on the stone of the crest. He slipped the silver star from its hiding place and pinned it to his shirt front, and waited.

Two horsemen bulged into the still white flood of the moonlight. One was a hard-looking individual Slade had never seen before, The other was gray — faced Howard Becker. They dismounted and walked to the very lip of the overhang, the hard-featured man carrying a bundle of something, and peered down.

Slade stepped into the silver blaze of the moonlight. His voice rang out. 'Elevate! In the name of the state of Texas! You are under arrest!'

Both whirled toward the sound of his voice, Becker's face that of a devil from the deepest hell. The other gave an astounded yelp, 'Goddermighty! He's a Ranger!'

Becker moved, and his shoulder draw was smooth and amazingly fast. The other also went for his gun.

Slade shot with both hands. The bundle-carrying man pitched forward onto his face. Becker fired even as the Ranger squeezed trigger again. Slade reeled sideways under a terrific shock. Lights blazed before his eyes. Bell notes stormed in his ears. Through a haze of blood and pain he dimly heard Becker's scream of terror as he lurched back and back and fell over the lip of the cliff. A second later the thud of his broken body drifted upward. This was the last sound Walt Slade heard before a wave of blackness engulfed him.

Overhead, the moon shone benignly, it's light bathing the motionless forms of outlaw and Ranger.

22

'When Slade recovered consciousness, his head was one vast ache, his face was caked with dried blood, his body was wet with dew and shivering with cold. After a prodigious effort, he assumed a sitting position and for a moment was frankly sick. Recovering somewhat, he managed to get to his feet, trying to still the chattering of his teeth.

'This won't do,' he muttered. Staggering to Shadow's thicket, he broke off some dry branches and started a fire over which he huddled until the warmth had thawed the chill from his bones.

Straightening up, he summoned enough strength to get the rigs off the two horses, leaving the animals to their own devices. A single glance at the outlaw's body assured him the sidewinder was satisfactorily dead. To heck with him! Sheriff Orton could look after him and the other. The bundle of dynamite which, fortunately, was not capped, he carefully laid aside to be picked up later.

'Now feller, it's up to you,' he told Shadow as he tightened the cinches, slipped in the bit and climbed to the saddle. 'Maybe we can make it to Hamon before we topple over.'

Shadow was at his best in an emergency. He negotiated the treacherous slopes, circled the hills and reached the canyon without mishap. Slade wasted but a single glance on Howard Becker's mangled form and rode on, lurching and weaving in the saddle, gripping the horn now and then for support. But by the time he reached Hamon, in the golden flush of the dawn, he had recovered sufficiently to properly care for the horse before shambling to Bije Manning's house and hammering on the door till the storekeeper appeared, lamp in hand.

'What in blazes?' Manning exclaimed. 'Come in! Come in!'

'Everything properly taken care of,' Slade replied. 'Tell you all about it later. No, I'm not badly hurt — just creased above the left temple. Shock knocked me cold for a while. Now I just want to wash up a bit and tumble into bed before I collapse. And Bije, send Orton a wire telling him to get here quick as he can.'

Bije Manning was deft at such matters, and after Slade washed the dried blood from his face, he swiftly padded and bandaged the wound, which he concluded was of little consequence. Then Slade weaved into his bedroom and in less than five minutes was sound asleep.

The sun was high in the sky when he awoke feeling much better. The bitter ache behind his eyes was gone, and although he was still stiff and sore from exposure, he was ready for anything. Dressing, he descended to the living room, where he found Manning awaiting him.

'Your breakfast is ready and Orton is on his way,' the storekeeper said.

While he ate, Slade gave Manning an account of the night's happenings. The storekeeper shook his head in bewilderment. 'Becker!' he exclaimed. 'I'd never have thought it. He sure did cover up wonderfully.'

'Yes, he was shrewd,' Slade agreed. A resourceful and able man who somehow took the wrong fork in the trail. Why? That's a mystery, one I have never been able to explain. Well, still there thunders down through the centuries, 'The wages of sin is death!'

He was silent for a few moments, reviewing events and experiencing a feeling of quiet satisfaction. The C. & P. would win the race to Randal, and his chore was finished as it should be finished.

Sheriff Orton arrived shortly and the story was repeated for his benefit. He did not appear particularly surprised at the dramatic outcome.

'You're always at your best when the going looks hardest,' was his comment. 'Now what?'

Slade glanced at the sun. 'I think we can make it to the cliff-top before sunset,' he said. 'I wish you to see everything, including the bundle of dynamite they packed along to blow the overhang. We'll pick up the head foreman of the track layers on the way; I have things to show 'him and some instructions to give him.'

It was still some time till sunset when they reached the cliff crest. Slade pointed out salient features and told the foreman just what to do.

'Steel clamps and braces anchored deep in the stone will secure that overhang from the effects of frost and thaws and a possible lightning bolt,' he explained.

'Certain,' said the foreman, nodding his understanding. He produced a rule.

'I'll take a few measurements and set the machine shop boys at work forging the clamps,' he said.

The two horses had not left the crest, so the rigs were replaced and the outlaw's body secured to one. On the way back, Howard Becker's body was roped to the other.

'We'll pack 'em to Hamon and on to Oresta tomorrow,' Orton said. 'They can hold an inquest if they are of a mind to.'

When they reached Oresta the following day, the green and gold splendor of the Winona, General Manager Dunn's private car, was on the spur.

An astounded man was Jaggers Dunn when Slade regaled him with an account of the stirring happenings during his absence. He shook his head, brushed back his glorious crinkly white mane from his big dome-shaped forehead and swore fluently.

'Becker!' he concluded. 'Well, the scoundrel sure put it over on me. But he didn't put it over on you.'

'After all, sir, you are an empire builder, not a law enforcement officer,' Slade reminded him.

'Maybe so,' grunted Dunn, 'but at times I sure pick some faulty bricks. Well, I guess nobody is perfect at everything, though I figure you come close to it.

'I know there's no use asking you to accept something for all you've done for me, because you won't,' he added. 'But here's a little check made out to the fund you had set up to assist the dependents of Rangers killed in the line of duty. You can hardly refuse that.'

Slade's lips pursed in a soundless whistle as he read the amount of the general manager's check; he carefully stowed it away in an inside pocket, turned and gazed out the wide window.

Jaggers Dunn smiled slightly as he saw that *El Halcón's* eyes were resting on the far distant horizon, and beyond. 'Suppose you're on the move, now?' he said,

'Yes,' Slade replied. 'My work here is done and Captain Jim will very likely have something lined up for me by the time I get back to the post. *Adios!*'

★ ★ ★

Two days later, as she watched him ride away, tall and graceful atop his great black horse, off to answer the call of duty and to face danger and new adventure, Gypsy Carvel murmured softly to herself. 'The heart of a man to the open road! Yes. But perhaps after a while the lure will lessen, and then — maybe!'